GRANNY GOES WILD

A SECRET AGENT GRANNY MYSTERY BOOK 9

HARPER LIN

ONE

The fact that I stumbled across yet another murder while on a camping trip with my grandson came as a big surprise. Not that the murder was a surprise—they have been happening around me with such frightening regularity that I'm beginning to think I'm some sort of mild-mannered weapon of mass destruction. No, the real surprise was that I was able to tear Martin away from his phone for an entire three-day weekend.

I'm Barbara Gold. Age: 71. Height: 5′5″. Eyes: blue. Hair: gray. Weight: none of your business. Specialties: undercover surveillance, small arms, chemical weapons, Middle Eastern and Latin American politics. Current status: retired CIA agent, widow, and grandmother.

Addendum to current status: in the wilderness, cut off from phone coverage and with no idea where I am while trying to protect an adolescent boy from a murderer who's stalking us.

Perhaps I should back up.

My grandson Martin's school offered a parent/child hiking trip over the Labor Day weekend. My son and his wife signed him up without telling him, thinking (A) he'd like it, (B) it would give my daughter-in-law some much-needed alone time, and (C) it would be a good experience for him.

Assumptions A and B turned out to be incorrect.

When he heard that he wouldn't be allowed to take any electronic gadgets, including his phone, he set up a howl to frighten a thousand banshees. His parents, Frederick and Alicia, stood firm, however, saying it would be a "growing experience." That led Martin to explain that growing experiences were stupid ideas concocted by old people to control young people and keep them from having any fun.

So much for assumption A.

Then Frederick, who was supposed to go with him, fell down a flight of stairs while showing some potential clients around a house he was trying to sell them and got a hairline fracture on his ankle. Not the best sales tactic. They didn't buy the house, and he ended up in a cast. Alicia volunteered to go with Martin but then got called away to CERN in Europe because they had some sort of emergency with the supercollider that you need a PhD in some esoteric science to even understand, let alone solve.

There went assumption B.

Then Martin made a terrible assumption of his own: he figured that with his dad laid up on the sofa watching Westerns and his mom flying over the Atlantic, he wouldn't have to go.

It was then that I stabbed him in the back.

No, I didn't murder my grandson. The dead guy comes later.

I volunteered to take him on the trip myself.

"Whaaat?" all three of them said over the dining room table.

They all looked incredulous. Martin added appalled and betrayed to that emotion. They all stared at me—little, gray-haired old me—as if they couldn't imagine me on a hike in the mountains.

And it was true that I had never done any survival training in northern American woodland. Jungles and deserts were more my thing. I'd even clambered over a glacier or two.

Pro tip: don't fire your M16 on full automatic

while standing on a glacier. You shoot backward like an Olympic skater with a poor sense of direction

But I digress.

"Barbara... do you think you're up for it?" Alicia asked. "They're going to be hiking in some pretty remote mountains."

I only smiled. As remote as the Khyber Pass? Not in this state.

"I looked at the information sheet they sent," I replied. "The hikes are only eight miles a day, with a change in altitude of only a thousand feet. I used to run that."

Martin laughed. Alicia gave me one of those indulgent, pitying looks old people get from young people when they mention how they were once young too.

But then Frederick, bless his heart, stood up for me.

"She used to run a lot more than that. When she wasn't on one of her business trips, she'd go jogging ten miles with a backpack full of stones. Must have weighed fifty pounds."

"Eighty," I corrected.

"Grandma used to ruck?" Martin asked incredulously.

"Language!" I snapped at the boy.

He flushed. "*Rucking*. It's when you go around with a bag full of stones on your back."

"Oh," I replied. Now it was my turn to blush. I'd never heard that term. The new fitness gurus had come up with all sorts of flashy words for things we used to simply call "training."

"Your grandmother was in amazing physical health," Frederick said. "I never understood why she and my dad did so much training for a boring government job."

Boring? It was never boring. Terrifying? Yes, but never boring. But we had told Frederick we were a pair of federal pen pushers who had to go on regular tours of inspection.

Martin looked at me, puzzled. "That's cool, I guess. But that was, like, ages ago. When what's-his-name was president. Bush?"

"I worked under both Bush administrations. Clinton too."

"Like I said, ages ago."

Good thing I hadn't mentioned Carter. Or Ford. The boy probably didn't even know who they were.

"I'm still in good shape," I said. "The hikes will be easy."

"I don't think you'd like it," Martin said. "You

won't get to do your book club or see your boyfriend."

This last was said with a chuckle and a sly look at his dad, who frowned. Frederick still hadn't gotten used to the concept.

"I think she'd do fine," Frederick said, obviously liking the idea of getting me away from Octavian for a long weekend. He had caught us kissing once, and I think it traumatized him.

"They're really intense hikes," Martin said. "Like super-survival Special Forces stuff."

"Not really," Frederick countered. "And she's been doing power walking every morning. Haven't you, Mom?"

"I have. And I'll do some more every day until we go so that I'll be fit."

"Then it's decided," Frederick said with a note of triumph. Not only would he get a Labor Day weekend alone to drink beer and have his buddies over to watch sports and Westerns, but he'd keep me from kissing anyone for three whole days.

Martin groaned, defeated. Alicia gave me a concerned look.

I smiled at my grandson. "Don't worry. It's going to be fun. I love nature."

Martin made a gagging sound and looked away. I furrowed my brow, confused, and then it hit me.

On one of my previous cases, I'd had to infiltrate a naturist colony to catch a murderer, going under-cover (or uncovered, rather) as a naturist. Or nudist. Or nakedist. Or whatever you called them.

Martin had stumbled upon my membership card and nearly broke the state record for the youngest boy to have a heart attack. I had to quickly explain that I was working as a special deputy for the police department.

That had staved off Martin's existential crisis and earned me cool points, but it had remained hanging between us as a source of unspoken embarrassment ever since.

Luckily, this hike was not to a naturist resort. Instead, it was to a rural stretch of mountains out of reach of cell phone coverage.

I thought that sounded relaxing.

Martin thought it sounded boring.

Turned out we were both wrong.

TWO

"OK, Cheerville Campers, let's have a big cheer for what's going to be a super-duper-great weekend!"

The dozen teenagers from Martin's high school who had "volunteered" to go on this trip glared at the bright-eyed, smiling woman standing in front of us. She was about thirty, fit, tanned, and wearing a T-shirt sporting the logo of Muggy Mountains State Park, khaki shorts, and hiking boots. She smelled of mosquito repellent and unbridled enthusiasm.

"Hip hip hooray! Hip hip hooray! Hip hip hooray!" we all cheered.

"We" being Ms. Chipper and the assembled parents and lone grandmother. The teenagers did not join in.

Yes, Chipper was her actual name. Marjory

Chipper, the head P.E. teacher at Cheerville High School.

It was eight a.m. on a Saturday morning, a time most high school freshmen are winding down from a long night of texting and gaming, and we stood in the gravel parking lot at the entrance to Muggy Mountains State Park. Before us rose the wooded peaks of the Muggy Mountains. The leaves were just beginning to turn, and the green slopes were brightened by swaths of yellows and reds.

The mountains weren't terribly high, but there sure were a lot of them, stretching north and west for a good hundred miles. It was all state park except for a couple of places where coal mines had been given concessions to turn mountains into craters. I hoped none of those operations would be on our hiking route.

"We have a fan-fun-tastic three days ahead of us!" Ms. Chipper said. "We're going to start at the trailhead right over there and follow Benson's Creek for five miles until the trail takes us up and over Miner's Ridge. There, we'll see some old mining equipment and the entrances to some nineteenth-century mines. I'll be giving a lecture on the history of mining in this area—"

Groans from the teenagers. Not only did they get

woken up at this ungodly hour, but they had to endure a history lecture too?

"—then we'll hike three miles down the back side of Miner's Ridge and along Coal Valley to our first campsite. The next day, we'll go deeper into the wilderness, following Coal Valley for seven miles before going up the side of Widow's Peak and camping there for the night. The third day, we'll do a loop around the peak and come back here by a short-cut. Is everybody ready?"

The adults took that as a signal to cheer. The teens took that as a signal to act sullen. Someone farted. Martin giggled. Ms. Chipper pretended she didn't hear.

"Okaaay. So now here's the part you've all been waiting for, at least the parents have been waiting for." The P.E. teacher shot us a grin. "Everyone coming on the trip, hand over your cell phones, iPads, computers, and any other electronics to Mr. Bradford." She indicated Martin's history teacher, a red-eyed little man who stood to one side. "He'll keep all your devices safe and will meet us at the parking lot when we come out of the wilderness."

I imagined a mob of Internet-deprived teenagers swarming over the poor man, tearing him apart in their rush to grab their devices and start texting, gaming, sharing, uploading, downloading, emojiing, LOLing, and whatever else they did when they stared at the darn things twelve hours a day.

The teens stared at Mr. Bradford. Mr. Bradford stared back at the teens. It was like a Mexican stand-off. I could practically hear the Ennio Morricone music.

I decided to break the deadlock.

I pulled out my phone and walked over to him. "Here you go."

"Thank you," Mr. Bradford replied, wafting me with a cloud of last night's booze. Whiskey, from the smell of it, and not the good stuff either. Now that I was taking a look at him, he had quite the red nose and cheeks. He looked tired, too, with bloodshot eyes and slumped shoulders. He moved and spoke all right, so he was hungover, not drunk.

At least he wouldn't have a head-on collision as he drove home, scattering our phones all over the highway.

Still, he hardly acted like a good role model for these teenagers. I was glad he wasn't coming along.

The other adults started collecting phones and iPads from their moaning offspring. One teenaged boy put on a Southern accent and yelled, "You can have my phone when you pry it from my cold, dead fingers!"

"That can be arranged," his father said. The boy gave up his phone.

I went over to Martin. He stood amid his friends, looking mournfully at all those wonderful electronic gizmos moving into a big bag Mr. Bradford held out. Briefly, I wondered why they had bothered to bring their devices here at all when they knew they'd have to give them up. Then I remembered that they'd surely wanted to use them on the drive over. Deprive a teenager of a whole hour of texting while being driven to the middle of nowhere? Silly me.

When Martin saw me approach, he got a deer-in-the-headlights look. I gave him my best "Grandma loves you" smile and held out my hand. He rolled his eyes and gave me his phone, which I promptly gave to Mr. Bradford before he changed his mind, snatched it from me, and ran for the hills.

Then I noticed not every parent was giving their children's devices to the history teacher. Most were bidding their kids goodbye and getting into their cars.

"Where are they going?" I asked.

"Parents don't have to come if they sign a waiver," Mr. Bradford said. "Didn't you get one?"

I glanced at Martin, who started looking as shifty

as a used-car salesman trying to convince a potential customer that the bargain 2003 Lexus only has twenty thousand miles on it. Then I understood. He had removed that form from the package he'd had to take home, hoping that his parents wouldn't want to go, and thus he wouldn't have to. Never underestimate the low cunning of your average teenager.

"Okay, everybody ready?" Ms. Chipper asked in her most chipper voice. "Let's go see some nature!"

A dozen pairs of teenaged shoulders slumped in unison. The class shuffled toward the trailhead, accompanied by only three parents, including me, plus the P.E. teacher and the Cheerville High School photography teacher, who would be preserving the kids' happy experience for the yearbook. I breathed in the fresh air, adjusted my pack, and fell in beside Martin.

I had to admit that I felt a bit nervous. Despite my bravado, I was not in the peak condition that I used to be. There was a time when I could have done the three days' worth of hikes the school had planned in a single day, toting an M16 and a sixty-pound pack. But those days were far in the past. All those marches, all those fights had begun to catch up with me. Now I had various aches and pains and got tired far more easily than I used to.

It was a bit of a rip-off, I must say. I had been one of the most fit women in the CIA, and now I wasn't much better off than many senior citizens who had spent their lives sitting in front of the television and eating potato chips. I'd worn my body out.

Sadly, I had to admit, I had also let my body slip. After my husband died, I had stopped exercising entirely, and that had hastened my physical decline. You can't stop when you get to my age. The gym is just as important for people in their seventies as for people in their forties—perhaps more so.

For the past year, I'd been getting back into exercise, but had I recovered enough? This hike was a one-way trail going deep into the mountains, with no side trails to get us out quickly. If I ended up hurt or exhausted one day in, I'd have a very difficult time getting out.

Then there was the pinched nerve in my back. It had acted up a few months before, a new ailment coming out of nowhere right in the middle of a case. Luckily, I had discovered Mr. Chong, proprietor of Get To The Point Acupuncture. I'd never tried acupuncture before, but I figured a six-thousand-year-old civilization might know a thing or two, and it turned out that it did. A few sessions of looking like a porcupine had made me as good as new.

But as far as I knew, Mr. Chong didn't have an office in the Muggy Mountains. If my back acted up, I'd be in serious trouble.

I set those worries aside. In the CIA, we always said that you should only worry about the things you could control. I'd maintain a steady pace, watch where I stepped, keep myself fed and hydrated, and leave the rest up to fate.

But as it had many times in my career, fate decided to play some tricks on me.

THREE

The first few miles were easy and pleasant. We followed a clear trail along a burbling creek as birds twittered in the trees. The air was rich and moist, full of forest smells. The temperature was in the low seventies, although the humidity made me sweat a bit. I noticed the area was fairly thick woodland, with a fair degree of underbrush that reduced visibility, perfect for setting up an ambush. From what I could see through occasional breaks in the trees, the valley had steep sides with many gullies and plateaus, perfect for mortar emplacements. I tried to turn off my military mindset and simply enjoy my surroundings. The chances that anyone would want to shell our little group of hikers with a mortar were slim to none.

The trail was narrow enough that we walked single file, at least the adults. The kids all paired up. Martin quickly abandoned his backstabbing grandmother, the cause of all his present troubles, and walked beside a girl I heard him call Melanie. They kept up a constant chatter, looking at each other more than where they were going.

Nature played a cruel trick on teenaged boys. Just as they began to find girls as interesting as or even more interesting than baseball or television, they developed pimples all over their faces. Martin's complexion wasn't as bad as most, but he had a real honker right on the side of his nose that looked just about ripe for popping. Several smaller spots created a constellation across his beardless chin.

Nature didn't leave it at that. As we all knew, girls matured faster than boys, and while Martin was still a bit gangly and childlike, Melanie had bloomed into young womanhood and stood a good inch taller than Martin.

That didn't stop Martin from trying to impress her.

"Oh, this trail is going to be easy," he said, trying to make his voice go low like a man's. "I run five miles a day. This year, I'm on the track and field team."

His voice cracked right at the end, ruining the effect. He ended up saying "track and fIIEEeeeld."

Did I detect the faint trace of a mocking smile on Melanie's lips? *Watch it, you little hussy—only Martin's parents and I are allowed to make fun of his voice cracking!*

The valley narrowed until it ended in a steep ridge. The creek we'd been following was actually a spring that shot out of a spot in the ridge about ten feet above our heads, a truly stunning sight. Everyone stopped to take pictures, or at least tried to. That was a sight to behold too. Twelve kids all reached into their pockets in unison to retrieve phones that were no longer there. Twelve faces fell. Twelve young throats let out grumbles. At least three voices cracked.

"Pity we can't take a photo," one of the parents said. He was Quinten Long, a bespectacled little man with a bad case of allergies whom I recognized as one of the librarians at the Cheerville Municipal Library.

"It was your idea to go on this dumb trip, Dad," said one of the boys. He was a big brute of a kid, taller and heavier than his father, who wore a jersey for the Cheerville High football team.

Quinten cringed.

"Don't worry, I'll take some shots," said the photography teacher, pulling out an expensive 35mm camera and snapping a few shots. Some of the students gathered around, attracted to the only electronic device within ten miles like cats to an open tin of tuna.

"Barbara, would you like to pose in front of the waterfall?" the teacher asked. His name was Thomas Cardiff. I'd met him before.

Thomas knew me from a story he'd done for the *Cheerville Herald*, where he worked part time as a photographer. The *Herald* was a thin little sheet that only came out weekly. Nobody worked full time at the *Herald*. I had acted in a small role in a movie filmed in town, and he had done an article on me.

That hadn't sat well with me. I liked to keep a low profile, but there had been no way out of it. I had insisted that I be photographed in costume to make myself less recognizable and that the article did not appear on the paper's website.

Thomas motioned his camera toward the waterfall and gave me an encouraging look.

"Oh, all right." I grabbed Martin and made him pose with me. I smiled. Martin put on one of those

"I'd rather be anywhere else" smiles. Thomas snapped away. Then he asked several others to pose.

I sat on a log and took off my pack, enjoying the scene. While it would have been more tranquil if the kids hadn't been there, running around and splashing each other, I felt glad they were. Too many young people (and old people, for that matter) spent all their time in cities or suburbs and never got out to see the beauty this world had to offer. It was a pity. I promised myself to come out to the country more often. I wondered if Octavian would like to come along.

"Are you all right, Grandma?"

Martin and Melanie stood beside me. I hadn't even noticed them.

"Oh, yes, just enjoying myself."

"You're not tired or anything?" he asked.

"No, I'm fine."

At first, I thought he was looking for an excuse to return to the parking lot, but then I saw actual concern on his face. I resisted the temptation to kiss him on the forehead. Melanie might give him another of those condescending smiles.

"I'm as fit as a fiddle," I assured him.

Ms. Chipper's voice rang out over the sound of splashing water. "Okay, everybody, time to climb

Miner's Ridge. Packs on, chins up, and pucker those lips for some good, old-fashioned whistling!"

True to her word, she set off along the trail, whistling a merry tune.

"Is she going to be like this the whole way?" Melanie grumbled.

"I hope not," I said.

The girl gave me a smile. Martin cut in and started chattering with her again, and I guessed my interaction with her was over.

The trail grew steep, with many switchbacks. I kept up, though, thanks partially to the school photography teacher, who was huffing and puffing and had turned as red as a tomato. The poor fellow slowed everyone down. He didn't look all that out of shape, perhaps in his early forties and not over-weight, but if one lives a sedentary life, any sort of physical exertion can be tough.

About a third of the way up, we came to our first abandoned mine.

It stood just a little off the trail, a roughly square hole in the side of the hill, about five feet to a side. Rotten boards crisscrossed the entrance, and a faded state government sign warned of dangers and a big fine for going inside.

"Coool," one of the boys said. Everyone nodded.

We all went over to look except for Thomas, who plunked down on the trail and pulled out his canteen.

"I don't think we should go close to it," said one of the parents, a woman named Angie, who was the mother of one of the girls. "It doesn't look safe."

"It's safe as long as we're careful," Ms. Chipper said, getting between the kids and the entrance. "This is one of the many disused mines in the area. From the middle of the nineteenth century to just a few short decades ago, hardy prospectors came here to mine the lead that can be found in the Muggy Mountains. Our state was the fifth-biggest producer of lead in the country."

Someone made a snoring noise. I had to admit that I wasn't particularly impressed by this fascinating historic fact either.

"Can we go in?" Martin asked.

"Nope, nope, and three times nope. It's against the law for a reason—actually, several reasons. The main one is that these mines are dangerous. The miners were prospectors, regular folk who wanted to strike it rich in the lead rush. Most didn't know how to construct a mine properly, and many died in cave-ins. Now some of these mines are more than a hundred years old, and they're very unstable. But we can take a peek."

"Don't get too close," Angie said, standing well back. She tried to stop her daughter, but the girl slipped away to join the crowd.

Ms. Chipper pulled out a flashlight and shined it through the boards. Everyone took turns peering inside. The flashlight illuminated about thirty feet of a shaft gently sloping downward. Timber frames haphazardly held up the walls and ceiling, although in a few spots, they had fallen out of place. Heaps of rocks were testimony to minor cave-ins. Near the end of the lit area, I saw an old rusted pickaxe and what looked like a bucket, now turned into a tangle of rotted wood and a couple of rusted hoops.

"Why, it's just like the old miner left it," I said, leaning forward to try and get a better look.

A board splintered under my hand, and I staggered back. A good quarter of the barrier crumbled into a pile of rotten wood at my feet.

"Grandma!" Martin said, embarrassed.

The kids laughed.

"Hey, Martin, your grandma is going to get arrested for breaking and entering," one of the boys joked.

It wouldn't be the first time, I thought as I brushed my hands clean.

"If they want us to stay out of these mines, they should board them up better," Martin said.

"I agree," I replied, checking for splinters.

"Budget cuts," Ms. Chipper said. "And that means we have to be extra-super careful. Okay, folks, let's hump this ridge!"

That got a bunch of snickers from the teens. Ms. Chipper, oblivious, strode on up the trail. The teens and parents fell in behind her, Angie warning everyone to be careful of mineshafts and pythons (pythons?), the huffing and puffing photographer taking up the rear.

We made our camp on the other side of the ridge in a lovely glade that was one of the only level spots in the narrow canyon we found ourselves in. We could see several boarded-up mineshafts on the slopes nearby.

I set up my tent, purchased from Megaton Army Surplus, in less time than anyone else, much to everyone's amazement. Then I helped several people sort out poles, pegs, and tarps, and soon, we got everything in order. Quinten's son set up their tent while his father tried to help and only succeeded in getting in the way. Ms. Chipper helped out the rest of the kids. It seemed we were the only two adults who had ever slept outdoors. Once we got everyone squared away, I set up the rest of my little camp, including a sleeping bag and an inflatable mattress to put under it. I was taking no chances with my tricky back.

The mattress gave me some trouble. It took a lot of breaths to get it inflated. I should have affixed it to the photographer's mouth while he was hiking. Although on second thought, that might not have been a good idea. He might have blown it up so much that both mattress and photographer would have drifted away on a strong breeze.

In the end, Martin took time away from his friends to help me. I resisted the urge to tousle his hair and kiss him. That would have earned me the silent treatment for the rest of the trip.

Ms. Chipper turned out to be a good hike leader. Once everyone had settled down, she broke out some hot dogs to roast over a blazing campfire. Of course, the boys all made jokes about "hot wieners" and left them over the fire too long so flames shot up from them. Then they dueled with the torches. The girls found a squirrel's cache of acorns and started pelting the boys, which made them chase the girls with flaming wieners. Angie cried out that they were all going to get burned, and Quinten complained that all the running around was blowing smoke in his face. Ms. Chipper mildly chided them but mostly let them do what they wanted.

My estimation of her went up. The kids really seemed to be enjoying themselves now, and she didn't want to spoil their fun. While this trip probably wouldn't make avid outdoor adventurers out of any of them, it would at least give them some fond childhood memories and show them there was a world beyond their school and phones.

The only person who didn't seem to be enjoying himself was Thomas Cardiff, the photographer. He huddled close to the fire, peering out into the darkness.

"What's wrong?" I asked after a couple of hours of this.

"I hear movement out there."

"I'm surprised you can hear anything over this racket."

"It's hardly a peaceful sojourn in the wilderness," Quinten grumbled, cleaning his glasses.

Just then, his son came whooping past, swinging a blazing marshmallow. Quinten flinched. "Watch it, Butch!"

Butch ended up on top of a rock, pounding his

chest and doing a good imitation of a gorilla. I had heard he was the team's star linebacker, even though he was their youngest member. Puberty came quicker in some than others. The kid even looked as if he shaved regularly.

The excitement and the sugar high could only last so long. Gradually, the teens began to settle down, pleasantly worn out by a day of fresh air, exercise, and the lack of artificial light and technological distractions. One by one, they yawned, stretched, cracked a few final jokes, and slumped off to their tents. Martin went to his own tent, and I decided it was time I got some sleep. I checked my watch. It was only nine thirty.

The other adults decided to turn in too. Ms. Chipper threw dirt over the fire, and the campground grew dark.

With my inflated mattress and sleeping bag, I felt quite cozy and comfortable, and I soon drifted off to sleep.

That sleep did not last long.

"AAAAGH!"

A scream tore me to wakefulness. I reached for my 9mm to find that it wasn't there. A moment later, I woke up enough to know why—I was on a school hike and hadn't brought it along, since it was a felony to bring a firearm into a state park. I hadn't thought it necessary anyway. Now I wasn't so sure.

Because that scream hadn't come from one of the kids fooling around but from an adult.

A man, to be precise.

FOUR

I stumbled out of my tent. The first thing I saw was a flashlight bobbing nearby.

"Look!" Thomas's voice shouted.

I saw it just as he was saying it. On a nearby hill, a fire blazed. It looked like the letter H.

"What in the world is that?" I asked. It certainly didn't look like a natural forest fire.

Thomas stumbled over to me, trying to buckle his jeans while holding his flashlight at the same time.

"I came out here to, um, see the stars when I noticed that."

"Well, you didn't have to scream," Quinten said, crawling out of his own tent with a flashlight in hand. "You woke me up."

Thomas had woken all of us up. Everyone stood

and stared at the blazing letter, illuminating a hill about two or three miles away.

"I told you I heard someone moving around the woods," Thomas said, his voice trembling.

"Well, that's just terrible," Ms. Chipper said, sounding negative for the first time on the trip. "It's irresponsible and dangerous to let a campfire go out of control like that. This is a state park."

I wondered what sort of camper would build a fire in the shape of an H.

"It's going to start a forest fire!" Angie wailed. "We'll all be burned alive."

"I doubt it," Ms. Chipper said. "The forest is pretty damp, what with the rains we've been having."

Sure enough, the fire soon died down. Actually, it died down remarkably quickly, as if someone had set it with gasoline or some other agent instead of firewood, which would have lasted longer. Within a couple of minutes, all we could see was a faint trace of the letter as the twigs and leaves on the forest floor smoldered for a time. Soon, that, too, faded away.

"We need to leave," Angie said.

"Why?" one of the kids asked.

"Because the fire is going to scare the pythons off the hill and right over our camp."

"What's with the pythons?" I asked.

"This whole forest is crawling with pythons," Angie declared.

"I'm pretty sure it isn't," I said.

"Pythons only live in the Arctic," one of the kids said.

"Did you fail biology?" Martin asked.

"Okay, folks, let's all get back to bed," Ms. Chipper said. "Hopefully the park rangers spotted that and will track down the culprits. They deserve a big ol' fine and a zillion hours of community service."

She got back into her tent. One by one, everyone else followed suit. I lingered. So did Thomas.

I turned to him. "Why was it in the shape of an H, I wonder?"

I couldn't see his face behind the glow of his flashlight.

"Couldn't tell you," he replied curtly and went off to bed.

The next morning, we headed out early after a pancake breakfast over an open fire. Everyone was in high spirits except for Quinten, who complained he had a sore back from a rock beneath his tent, and Thomas, who didn't look like he had slept a wink. As we left the campsite, the photographer glanced several times at the H-shaped burn mark on the hillside.

Ms. Chipper reminded us that the plan for the day was to follow Coal Valley for seven miles before going up the side of Widow's Peak and pitching our tents at a campsite on its slopes.

"It will be a super-duper view," she said. "I just hope the weather holds out. If it doesn't, we'll just have to hunker in the tents and tell ghost stories."

To the south, the blue sky was lined with gray. The local TV station had predicted fine weather for the entire long weekend, but this wouldn't be the first time the forecasters had been wrong. Or the millionth.

So far, my body was holding up. The air mattress had been a good investment, and except for the previous night's brief interruption, I had slept like a baby. Fresh air and exercise will do that for you. My back felt fine, and nothing else hurt, although I did feel a bit fatigued. I figured once I was on the trail, I'd loosen up and get into the rhythm of the day.

I took it easy, staying near the back of our little group. Ms. Chipper led the way, and Thomas Cardiff, being the only other teacher, took up the rear, which was his natural place what with all his huffing and puffing. He kept looking over his shoulder.

"Everything all right?" I asked.

"Oh, I'm just making sure we don't have any stragglers."

"Like M&M?" one of the girls in front of us asked. The girl walking next to her giggled. They gave me a sly look then giggled again. It took me a minute to figure out.

M&M. Martin and Melanie. They'd been all but inseparable since the beginning.

Half a mile later, the trail straightened enough that I could see them, right at the front behind Ms. Chipper, holding hands.

Well, not exactly holding hands. They had hooked their pinky fingers together, which was even more adorable.

"Do you have a zoom lens?" I asked Thomas.

"Huh?" He had been looking over his shoulder again.

"No stragglers. See? You can count them. Do you have a zoom lens?"

"Sure."

"Could you get a photo of those two?" I pointed.

Thomas smiled. He didn't need to be told who I meant. They were just cresting a little hill. Thomas stopped and took a few snaps. He showed me the result on the screen at the back of the camera.

"Nice," I said. "Just don't put those in the year-book. They'll kill you."

Thomas muttered something and looked at the ground as he walked.

We continued up the trail as the sky turned leaden. I wasn't overly concerned about any rain, because Martin and I both had raincoats. Presumably everyone else had brought them, too, since they were on the list the school had sent out.

The trail cut along the eastern slope of Coal Valley, with trees uphill and below us. A few birds circled, level with us, before dipping out of sight to grab whatever mice or other small creatures they had spotted down there. The air cooled and smelled of rain.

The changing weather didn't seem to dampen the kids' spirits. They were all chattering away or darting off into the woods to chase each other. Angie kept calling them back, warning about pythons. Ms. Chipper called them back, too, if they strayed too far.

"Pythons you don't have to worry about. There are more mines in this area, though."

"Can we go in one?" Martin asked.

"We already had that conversation," Ms. Chipper said.

"Just one," Martin insisted. "And not very far."

"Barbara," Ms. Chipper called down the line. "You need to clean out your grandson's ears. Go find a sharp stick and swirl it around inside. Root out all that wax."

I snapped her my most military salute, which raised the eyebrows of a couple of the kids who saw me. Stepping away from the path a bit, I found a suitable stick and approached Martin in a fencing pose. My grandson cracked a grin then looked sidelong at Melanie and made a show of rolling his eyes.

"Don't be embarrassing, Grandma."

Thoroughly deflated, I followed "M&M" down the trail. They picked up speed to put a few people between me and them.

Rain began to patter down in big, heavy drops. Everyone donned their rain gear.

"I hope it doesn't flood," Angie said.

"Then we'll have to worry about water moccasins," I said.

Her eyes widened. "You think?"

"No."

"Time for a head count," Ms. Chipper said now that the column had stopped and bunched up as everyone changed for the weather. She began to count, dramatically bopping each person on the head with a fingertip.

"Where's Thomas?" she asked.

Everyone shrugged.

"Mr. Cardiff always walks at the back to make sure no one gets left behind," one of the kids said.

"Yes, but now it looks like he got left behind," Ms. Chipper said.

"I'll go look for him," I announced. He had been acting strangely, and I had grown curious.

"You shouldn't go alone," Quinten said, moving to join me. His glasses were fogged and covered in raindrops.

"Can you see?" I asked.

"Of course I can see. Why do you ask?"

I shrugged. "Let's go."

We found Thomas just five minutes down the trail, around a sharp bend that took us to a fine lookout over Coal Valley. He stood on a rock, pointing his camera down the length of the valley, back the way we came. We had been following a gentle slope uphill toward Widow's Peak, which stood swathed in fog.

"Oh, he's just taking a picture," I said.

"Who?" Quinten asked, tripping over a root and nearly falling flat on his face.

"Thomas."

"You see him?"

"Right there." I pointed.

"Oh, yeah."

"Get a good photo?" I called out.

He jumped a little and turned. "Oh, it's you."

"Hello to you too. Angie is worried you got eaten by pythons."

"No, just trying to get a good photo."

"Not the best weather for it," I said.

"No." He put his camera away. "Sorry I slowed everybody down."

He moved up the trail. I hesitated a moment. Thomas had not been pointing his camera at the center of the valley, as if to take a picture of the valley as a whole, but rather toward one side of the valley, and he had his big zoom lens out at maximum.

I looked where I estimated he had been focusing. The trail ran like a brown ribbon along the wooded slopes. I couldn't see anything unusual.

"We should catch up with the others," Quinten said.

Thomas passed us. "Sure. Let's go."

We went around the bend. Thomas was just disappearing around another bend up ahead, walking more quickly than he had all day. On instinct, I stopped and told Quinten, "I dropped something back there. I'll catch up."

"All right," the librarian said and continued up the path.

I got to the bend and tried to hug the edge of the path, where a few overreaching branches and shrubs partially obscured me from sight. I stopped once I got a good view down the path and looked.

For a full minute, I stood, staring, although I did not know what I was staring at other than an empty path that grew more and more obscure as the rain began to fall more heavily. My eyes weren't what they used to be, and conditions weren't good.

But I could have sworn I saw something.

Under the shadow of a tree whose branches overhung the trail about a mile behind us, and about where Thomas had been pointing his camera, I thought I could discern a shape.

The shape of a person.

I could not say for certain that what I was seeing was an actual human figure or a tree trunk or even a trick of the shadow.

The best thing to do in that situation was to keep on looking.

The shape did not move.

A prickle ran over my skin. Being higher up and on a more sparsely vegetated stretch of the trail, I was probably much more visible than whatever it was I was trying to look at. My bright-red raincoat certainly didn't help.

I should have gotten a camouflage poncho at Megaton Army Surplus, but I hadn't wanted to embarrass my easily embarrassed grandson, and I hadn't seen any need.

Now I wondered.

The figure, if figure it was, remained motionless. I began to think I was staring at a tree. We had passed a few trees that had died and fallen over, leaving only a stub of the trunk, as well as a couple of blackened trunks from trees that had been split by lightning. It could very well have been one of those.

Still, I waited. Thomas obviously thought it to be of some interest, and that blazing H from the night before had certainly spooked him.

"Barbara!" Quinten called. His voice echoed down the valley. I wondered how far it would be audible.

"Quiet," I grumbled.

"Barbara, are you coming?" Quinten called from closer this time. I heard a thud and a quiet "ow."

Making a very teenaged eyeroll (I had spent too much time with high school freshmen), I walked quickly back up the trail and found Quinten picking himself off the ground.

"Lots of roots and rocks and things," he said once I got close enough for him to make me out through his fogged glasses. "They should clean this place up."

"Nature can be very inconsiderate at times."

The rain continued at a steady downpour. The column grew silent, leaving me to my thoughts. I told myself I was just being paranoid, that all those years in the CIA had made me jumpy. My attempt at self-reassurance did not last long, however. I caught Thomas glancing over his shoulder more than once, and I could not get that blazing H out of my mind.

"Something queer is going on here," I murmured.

The boy walking behind me snickered.

Oh dear. I really did have to watch my choice of words around the Zoomer generation. Everything was funny or ironic to them. I supposed it had been the same when I was fourteen, but to be perfectly honest, there had been too many gunfights and coups d'état since then for me to remember.

At the next rest break, Thomas went off to "take some pictures." I was trying to figure out an excuse to follow him when I noticed him scrambling up a boulder about twenty yards away that gave a commanding view of the valley. Butch, not to be outdone, climbed up too.

I sat down on a fallen log next to Martin, who

was alone at the moment as Melanie chatted with some of her friends.

"Nice to be without your phone for a while, isn't it?"

Martin rolled his eyes. "It's okay, I guess. I just hope Boozy Bradford doesn't lose it."

"I'm sure he'll take good care of it."

"He'll probably fall down on it or something," Martin said with a wicked grin.

A girl sitting nearby wrinkled her nose. "His breath stinks."

I couldn't argue with that, and since I didn't want to criticize a teacher in front of the kids, I said nothing. Instead, I watched Thomas and Butch on the boulder.

Butch thumped his chest and roared. His deep voice echoed across the valley.

I elbowed Martin. "Wouldn't it be funny if his voice cracked while he did that?"

My grandson and the girl laughed.

I smiled. Despite being passed over as poor company compared with Melanie, I was having a grand time, and the few moments I did get with Martin were proving to be fun.

Butch got on all fours and started howling like a wolf.

Thomas, standing right next to him, frowned but otherwise ignored him, scanning the valley behind us with his telephoto lens. He did not look as if he was trying to take a picture.

"Thomas, put that away," Ms. Chipper said. "Some of the girls and I have to go say hello to some ferns, if you know what I mean."

Thomas looked irritated but put his camera away and hopped off the boulder.

"I'll stay up here," Butch said.

"Oh, no you won't!" one of the girls shouted. Everyone laughed. Thomas held up a hand to the boy, who shrugged and jumped off himself.

Our camp that night was in a little fold on the side of Widow's Peak that gave us shelter from the wind but not the rain. Ms. Chipper solved this in her usual perky way by assigning two "monkeys" to climb the trees to fasten a tarp. Martin and Butch volunteered. While I would have liked to see one of the girls volunteer, I was still proud to see my grandson make it to the upper branch faster than Butch, who lacked Martin's agility—gained from endless hours at the skate park—and simply lumbered up with raw strength.

Within a minute, a large tarp was stretched above where we would set up the campfire, high enough that it wouldn't trap the smoke too badly and low enough that it would stop the rain from hitting the fire and the area right around it as long as the wind didn't angle the rain too much.

It was another raucous night, with Ms. Chipper trying and failing to get everyone to sing campfire songs. The kids mostly ignored the rain and chased each other around camp, pelting one another with pine cones, while the adults sat under the tarp, out of the incessant drizzle. Quinten had caught a cold and kept sneezing. Angie was convinced a flash flood would wash us off the mountain. Ms. Chipper warned the kids not to stray too far. An old mine stood a little up the slope, and she told the kids not to go near it.

Thomas looked glum, checking out some pictures on the screen on the back of his camera. When I tried to look, too, he put it away.

Eventually, we all went to bed. I felt a bit sorry that this would be my last night in the country with Martin.

If only.

For once again, I was awoken by a scream, but this time it wasn't Thomas who was screaming.

It was my grandson.

FIVE

"Help!" Martin shouted. "Mr. Cardiff has been hurt!"

Thomas? The photographer had been acting strangely since the first night. I scrambled out of my tent and straight into a heavy rain. I ducked back inside and grabbed my raincoat and flashlight.

When I got back out, the entire camp was in confusion. Several people had come out of their tents and were babbling all at once. A flashlight shined in my eyes, briefly blinding me before it moved elsewhere. I blinked and looked around.

"Martin! Where are you?"

A pair of flashlights came down the slope, wavering between the trees like will-o'-the-wisps. I shined my light in that direction and saw Martin and Melanie.

Both had terror stamped on their faces.

"What happened?" I said as I hurried over to them.

Martin was practically in tears. "We snuck off to see that old mine up the hill. When we got there, all the boards had already been pulled off, and Mr. Cardiff lay inside. I... I think he's..."

"He's dead!" Melanie wailed.

Ms. Chipper appeared. "You two stay here," she told them. "I'll go look."

She headed up the slope. Everyone started to follow. "No! No! All of you stay back."

"I know first aid," I said then turned to the others. "Quinten, Angie, take charge of the kids. All of you get into the center of camp and do a head-count. Turn on all your flashlights and shine them out of the camp to illuminate the area."

Quinten and Angie looked so shocked that they didn't even question these unusual instructions. I was already concerned for the camp's safety. Thomas had been afraid of something. If he had come to harm by other hands, it would be best if everyone stayed close together and lit up the area around the camp so that no one could approach unseen.

Ms. Chipper and I struggled up the slope. There was no trail, and our boots slipped on the wet leaves. We weren't even sure where exactly to find the mine in the dark, and we wasted an agonizing few minutes searching the slope before we found it.

Then we spotted it—a black, squarish hole in the slope.

As my grandson had said, the boards had all been removed and stacked neatly to one side of the entrance.

"Thomas?" Ms. Chipper called. I gritted my teeth at the sudden sound and shined my flashlight all around me.

The body lay facedown just inside the entrance. The blood matted in his hair glistened in the beams of our flashlights.

I shined my light down the mineshaft. It sunk at a slope down into the mountainside, a dank passageway about six feet to a side. Rotted wooden beams struggled to hold up the ceiling. Here and there, I could see evidence of small cave-ins.

Ms. Chipper knelt down by Thomas and shook him.

"My God," she gasped. "He's dead."

"Don't move him."

I studied the passageway again. Other than a few

spots just beneath Thomas's head, I saw no blood-stains as evidence that he had hurt himself—or been killed—at this spot. No spray of blood, no bloody stone or old pickaxe. Nothing. I studied the floor beyond the body. It had a heavy coating of dust and leaves that had blown in. There was a cluster of boot prints around poor Thomas, but they did not go more than a couple of feet farther into the passageway.

Trying not to disturb the scene, I measured one of the boot prints with my fingers and measured Thomas's boot.

The boot prints were bigger than his.

It became all too clear.

"He was murdered somewhere else and his body carried here. The killer hid his body in here, hoping no one would find it."

"Killed? Then... the killer might still be here. My God, the kids!"

She hurried out. While I wanted to stay to take a closer look at the scene, I followed. I could not leave her to make her way back to camp alone. That was what my son called Horror Movie Thinking. You let everyone go off one by one, and soon enough, you were the only one left alive.

As we made our way back to camp, I shined my

beam around again, looking for tracks. It was hard to see anything in the rain and the dark.

We stumbled back into camp and into chaos. Everyone was shouting, and Angie was beside herself, wailing to the kids that pythons had eaten their photography teacher. Quinten, practically blind behind his fogged and rain-beaded glasses, was trying to keep everyone calm and together but kept bumping into people. His son Butch was shouting for everyone to shut the bleep up or he'd bleeping pound them until they did. Martin and Melanie stood in the midst of all this, hugging each other and crying.

"Is everyone all right?" I asked. The question sounded stupid considering the circumstances.

Quinten understood what I meant. "We did a headcount. Everyone is accounted for."

"How did you count?" I asked. He wasn't even looking at me.

He turned to me at the sound of my voice. "I had them sound off."

"Good. Everyone, quiet down. We all need to stay calm."

"Thomas has been murdered!" Ms. Chipper wailed.

That did not help them stay calm.

Someone screamed, a couple of kids burst into

tears, and it took a good five minutes to get everyone quiet and organized.

"Yes, I'm afraid that's true," I said. "Now, the best thing we can do is stay here in camp until it's light."

"No way!" Angie cried. "Wait around here for the murderer to pick us off? We need to get out as soon as possible."

"We can't go running off into the dark with it raining this hard. Someone will slip and fall or get lost. The murderer isn't going to want to show himself. He's probably already snuck away. We don't want to meet him on the trail."

We huddled together under the tarp, cold and miserable. It was three hours until dawn. Several of the flashlights began to dim as their batteries drained. I tried to get the kids to save their batteries by turning their flashlights off, but no one dared.

I kept mine off, even though I had spare batteries in my pack. I had a feeling I'd need them.

Once everyone had calmed down a bit, Ms. Chipper and I took Martin and Melanie to one side.

"So tell me exactly what happened," I said.

Martin was too scared to lie and too scared even to worry about if he was going to get in trouble. He told me straight out. "I told Melanie we should go check out that abandoned mine. I had gone over to her tent to, like, talk after everyone went to sleep."

Martin and Melanie glanced at one another. Even in the dim light, I thought I could see the two of them blush. I wondered if anything other than talking had gone on. Probably not much more, but that was not the issue at the moment and none of my business anyway.

"Go on."

"We waited until we were sure everyone was asleep and snuck out. We had to wait for a while because we heard Mr. Cardiff cursing. We heard him walking around the camp, too, but he didn't have any flashlight on, just a bit of light from the campfire, and that was almost out."

"Was he talking to anyone?"

Melanie shook her head. "No, more like talking to himself. We couldn't really hear much of what he said other than the curse words, except for the very last thing he said, because he said it right outside our tent." She and my grandson exchanged glances. "I mean my tent."

"What did he say?"

"Something like, 'Fine, let's get it over with. I'll show you.' Then he walked out of the camp."

"And that's when you left?" Ms. Chipper asked.

"No," Martin said. "We were, like, worried we would bump into him. So we kinda hung out for, I don't know, another twenty minutes or so, and then we heard him come back. His tent is just across from ours, and we could see his flashlight through the side of our tent. I mean Melanie's tent. He unzipped his tent, kinda looked around inside for a bit, then turned off the flashlight and zipped up again. That's how we knew he had come back. We waited a few more minutes for him to go to sleep, and then we snuck out."

Poor Martin was too scared and confused to see the obvious: that hadn't been Thomas coming back, that had been the murderer. He had killed Thomas, dumped him in the mineshaft, and come to check on the tent.

I decided not to tell my grandson this. The poor child would figure it out soon enough.

So what had the murderer been looking for?

I went over to Thomas's tent. It was a pity that I couldn't try and track the murderer. Too many people had been stomping around here, and the rain, which was growing in strength, would wash away any tracks by the time it grew light.

Using a handkerchief, I pulled down the tent's zipper and shined my flashlight inside.

The interior was in disarray, as if it had been quickly searched. The sleeping bag had been thrown to one side and a few other items overturned. Thomas's pack was open, and I immediately saw what was missing—his camera and camera case. He had stored those in the top of his pack, where they would be protected from the elements but also easy to access. The rest of the pack's contents remained in place.

The murderer had wanted the camera and, as far as I could see, nothing else.

I felt a chill run through me. So Thomas really had been taking pictures of someone from that lookout point the day before. And that shape I had decided was a tree trunk had not been a natural feature of the landscape. It had been the killer.

The killer had been in camo or at least dark, natural colors. He had seen me, my red raincoat marking me out despite my being behind partial cover. He had stood motionless as I stared, waiting for me to think what I had thought—that there was nothing to see.

Ms. Chipper was peering over my shoulder.

"Do you see anything missing besides his camera?" I asked.

"Are you implying that I've been in his tent?"

"Have you?"

"No."

I shrugged, feeling slightly disappointed that only my grandson was guilty of tent hopping.

After zipping up the tent, I stood in the rain, apart from the huddled, frightened crowd, and asked the P.E. teacher some questions.

"Do you know anyone who would wish Thomas Cardiff any harm?"

She shrugged. "Not that I can think of. Well, he did get divorced last year, but his wife, can't remember her name, moved to Florida with a surfer dude. Scandalous. He couldn't have been more than twenty-five. Thomas was very bitter because he still had to pay alimony."

"Sounds like she got what she wanted," I muttered. "No reason for her to come back and kill him that I can see. What was the reason given for the divorce? If she was leaving him for another man and still got alimony, he must have done something bad to get the wrong end of the legal stick."

"She caught him going to the B&B."

"A bed-and-breakfast?"

"No, it's a strip club on the highway. It stands for—"

"Never mind. So he was going to a strip club, and

he was still allowed to teach high school?" I couldn't believe my ears.

"He never did anything inappropriate with the students. We've never had any complaints, and after we found out, we watched him like hawks, believe me. He was a sleaze, not a pervert."

"Hardly reassuring. I still don't see why he would be allowed to teach school. Call me old-fashioned, but I think teachers should act as moral role models for their students."

Ms. Chipper looked uncomfortable. "It's not that simple. You see, working at the newspaper, he had access to certain information."

"Such as?"

"Mr. Grundon, the principal of our school, has a bit of a past."

"Good Lord. What?"

Ms. Chipper raised a hand. "Nothing terrible. Just some tax dodging ten years ago."

"Oh, is that all?"

Yes, I know sarcasm is the lowest form of wit, but I couldn't help myself.

"He got fined," Ms. Chipper said. "Quite a big fine. So much of one that he had to sell his business. Mr. Grundon used to own a couple of houses that he rented to students near the university. This was before he was made principal. He then got a job teaching at our high school and worked his way up to being principal. Thomas was working at the newspaper back when Mr. Grundon got hit for tax fraud, and the paper planned to write a big article about it, but Mr. Grundon was friends with the mayor back then, and it all got hushed up."

"So how did you learn about it?"

"After Thomas got caught at the strip club, we had a staff meeting, and the principal threatened to fire him, so Thomas shot back with this information and said that if he got fired, he'd spread Mr. Grundon's dirty secret all over town."

"Charming."

Ms. Chipper shrugged. "He kept his job on the promise that he wouldn't go to any more strip clubs. We watched him carefully, but Thomas was on his best behavior. No trouble with the girls, or the boys for that matter."

I looked around, momentarily at a loss. While I had dug up some dirt on the victim, I could not see how this connected with his murder. This state of affairs had been going on for a year. I had also seen Mr. Grundon once when I had come to pick up Martin from school—a roly-poly little fellow who could not have climbed up and down these hills and snuck around our camp.

No, we were dealing with someone who was far more fit—and far deadlier.

And I had no idea who that someone was.

SIX

The day dawned gray and wet. The rain poured down now, gushing along every fold of the terrain to create countless little streams. The kids packed up their gear as quickly as they could, and the adults served out a cold meal. We weren't going to waste time cooking, not if there was a chance a murderer was around.

We hesitated when it came to taking down Thomas's tent.

"It's part of a murder scene," Quinten said. "We should leave it untouched."

"With all this rain, any fingerprints would have washed off," Ms. Chipper said.

"Could we just *go*?" Angie interjected.

"Quinten is right," I said. "We should leave it

here. Fingerprints might have washed off the outside, but there might still be evidence on the inside."

Ms. Chipper turned to the group of students. "Get everything together. We head out in five minutes!"

She was no longer her chipper self. Now she was serious, all business, and keeping a remarkably level head despite the circumstances. I liked her better this way.

"You said we were going to take a shortcut out of here," Quinten said. "How long before we get to civilization?"

Ms. Chipper pulled out a map of the state park. The trails were clearly marked. "This is the route we took coming in. As you can see, we took a rather circuitous path, stopping to see those mines and go to various vista points here, here, and here. Our return route is more direct, just going straight along here. It's nine miles, and it's almost all downhill except for passing over a couple of ridges. We can be out in a few hours. From there, I'll use the pay phone to call Mr. Bradford."

"You don't have your phone with you?"

"No, I didn't bring it so I could be an example to the students. Besides, there's no signal here anyway."

I looked back up the slope, where the entrance to the mineshaft was barely visible amid the greenery.

"I want to take another look at the body," I said.

"What?" Angie exclaimed. "We need to get out of here."

"I didn't get a good look at it in the dark last night. If we leave it now, there's a chance the murderer will return and get rid of evidence. We owe it to poor Thomas to recover as many details as we can. I'll take some photos of the crime scene for the police."

Ms. Chipper stared. "With what?"

"Oh, right. I don't have my phone either. Strange how we've become so reliant on the things."

"We need to go," Angie insisted. Her voice was taking on the knife-edge of panic.

"You need to go," I told her. "And so do the kids. All of you, get going. I'll catch up. The trail is easy enough to follow."

Ms. Chipper looked me over. "You're not going to catch up."

I was about to object but then realized she was right. "Then I'll just have to hike out on my own."

"I'll stay with you," Quinten said. "You shouldn't be alone."

I felt flattered by his courtesy, although I didn't see how he could be much help.

"I don't want to go without you, Dad," Butch whined. Although he was such an oversized young all-star, I suddenly saw vulnerability there.

"And I don't want to go without you," Martin told me.

"The students have to stay with me," Ms. Chipper insisted.

"Martin is my responsibility, and Butch is Quinten's. You can't be held accountable. And it's better if we have a group. The killer won't want to face us in a group."

"Yeah, and he's probably miles away by now anyway," Martin said.

I hoped that was true.

Ms. Chipper sighed, looked back at the anxious cluster of students, looked at me, and said, "All right. Take Thomas's map. He put it in the side pocket of his backpack."

I checked in his tent. "It's gone. But this changes nothing. You already pointed out the trail to me, and it's well marked. We'll be fine."

Ms. Chipper looked as if she would rather jump off a cliff than leave us, but she saw the sense in what I was saying. We couldn't just leave a murder scene unattended. I'd rather have waited until help arrived, but that might not happen before dark, and I didn't want to spend another night in the wilderness, not with that killer on the loose.

Reluctantly, Ms. Chipper gathered up the kids, as well as a frantic Angie, and headed out, but not before Martin and Melanie had a heartfelt farewell. The rest of the kids were too frightened to tease them, and they were too earnest even to notice what their peers did, much less care.

First, we took a close look in and around the camp but found nothing. While the surrounding brush was trampled in numerous places, most or all of those spots had probably been made by the kids themselves. We found nothing except a couple of candy wrappers, which, to my surprise, Martin picked up and put in his pocket.

"People should leave nature alone," he declared.

We headed up to the mineshaft, looking for clues all the while.

Once again, we found nothing. It had been raining heavily for hours, and it didn't look like it was going to let up anytime soon. If the murderer had left any traces, they were long gone now.

Not so in the mineshaft. It had been left, as far as I could tell, just as it had been the previous night.

The boards stacked near the entrance remained where we had discovered them. Telling the kids to keep back, because they were far too young to see a dead body, especially that of one of their teachers, Quinten and I went to the entrance.

The body still lay facedown just inside the entrance. The blood in his hair had dried, and his limbs had stiffened with rigor mortis. The boot prints in the dust had faded a bit, no doubt from the strong breeze that had blown all night, but remained fairly visible.

"I wish I could measure these prints before they fade away entirely," I muttered.

"What prints?" Quinten asked.

"Clean your glasses."

"Do you have a sewing kit?" He asked, pulling out a cloth and wiping his lenses clean. He put them back on, and the fog slowly began to form on them again.

"Yes. Why?"

Quinten sneezed. "Measure the boots with thread and cut them to size. Then you can give the thread to the police, and they'll have the measurements."

I gaped at him. "That's brilliant."

Quinten smiled. "Librarians are the unsung geniuses of our civilization."

"You're far too modest," I said, going to my pack and fetching my sewing kit as well as a ballpoint pen and notepad. The boys stood a little way off, water dripping off the hoods of their raincoats, looking around nervously.

I measured the boot prints as Quinten had suggested and cut the thread to the proper lengths. I took measurements of the boot length and maximum and minimum width and made a sketch of the pattern of the sole.

Once I finished, I checked the body again.

The blow was on the left-hand side of the skull, as if a right-handed man had swung some blunt, heavy object. Studying the wound, I could see he had been hit more than once. I imagined that he had been struck once, had fallen down, and then his attacker had struck him a couple of more times to make sure he was dead.

What was interesting, though, was that the blow was on the side of the head and slightly toward the front. Thomas had been facing his attacker when he got hit.

And yet we hadn't heard him cry out.

What had Martin and Melanie overheard him say? *"Fine, let's get it over with. I'll show you."*

I examined his clothes. His wallet was in his pocket, but it was jammed in at an odd angle, as if the killer had pulled out the wallet and then stuffed it back in haste. Using a handkerchief, I pulled it out and opened it. It was awkward work looking through it while trying not to leave any prints. The money, ID, and credit cards were there. It was a cloth wallet with two small pockets secured with zippers. Both were open and empty.

After returning the wallet to its place, I shined my light down the mineshaft and saw no evidence that the killer had gone farther than a few feet inside the shaft. He had obviously done away with Thomas at another location, dragged him here, and dumped him.

Dragged? Perhaps not. Dragging a body would have left a big mark in the forest, one that even a night of rainfall probably wouldn't erase. Had he carried the body? That would make him a strong man. I estimated Thomas to weigh about 180 pounds. Carrying him up a wet slope in the rain would have taken quite a lot of strength and balance.

Had there been more than one murderer?

I came out of the mineshaft to find Martin bending over the boards stacked near the entrance.

"Martin! I told you not to come close."

"Look, Grandma." He pointed to one of the boards.

On a hooked nail was a clump of thread, slicked down onto the wood by the rain. I looked closer and saw it was brown wool. Torn from a sweater the killer was wearing? Thomas hadn't been wearing brown wool.

"Good job, Martin!"

"Is that a clue?" He sounded happy to have helped.

"I do believe it is."

The boy grew serious. "That's from the killer, isn't it?"

"Probably."

"It was him we heard coming into camp, wasn't it? For a while, I thought it was Mr. Cardiff coming back. I wasn't thinking straight."

"It's all right. I know you were upset." I tried to give him a hug, and for the first time in a long time, he pulled away.

"We don't have time for that." He had a hard look on his face.

I blinked. For a moment, he looked like James,

my late husband. He had gotten that look any time the mission got tough. The "I'm scared and I'm hurting but I'm going to pull through" look.

I had never seen that look on my son Frederick. We had sheltered him from the hard things of the world, and he had grown up carefree and kind and (I must admit it) a bit soft. Martin had enjoyed that same life.

Until now.

It made me wonder how Frederick would have reacted if he had been here.

"You're right, Martin. Now that we've collected all the clues we can, there's nothing more we can do to help your teacher. Now we have to hike as fast as we can out of here and report to the police."

He nodded, eyes vulnerable, and looked at me for a long moment. I could see he really wanted that hug. And I really wanted to give him that hug.

But perhaps he didn't need it. Perhaps, at least for today, he had to be a man and not a boy.

"You better collect that bit of fluff," he said. "It might wash away in the rain."

"Yes, I think you're right."

I collected it, and after searching around the mineshaft and finding nothing, we headed back down to the abandoned campsite and followed the group down the trail.

We weren't far behind, only about half an hour, so I hoped that if we pushed hard, we might catch up.

The trail hugging the side of Coal Valley sloped gently downhill, and we made good time. Not as good as I would have liked, because the rain kept up, and the way at times was slippery, but I felt confident that if we did not catch up to the others, at least we would be out of the park well before nightfall.

We came to the scenic overlook where Thomas had been spying with his zoom lens. I peered down at the spot he had been focusing on. While it was hard to tell with the rain obscuring everything, I certainly didn't see any tree trunk where I thought I had seen one before.

Brown wool. Brown tree trunk. Yes, I had seen him, hadn't I?

I suppressed a little shiver.

"Look," Butch said, pointing down the valley.

Far in the distance, I could see the rest of the group on the trail. They were moving fast. Ms. Chipper had kept them going at a good pace. I bet Angie had helped with that too.

Butch and Martin started jumping up and down, shouting, and waving their arms.

"Who are you shouting at?" Quinten asked.

After a moment, one of the kids in the rear of the column pointed at us. The whole group stopped. Ms. Chipper appeared and waved to us. We waved back. They did not move.

"Good, they're waiting for us," I said.

"Who?" Quinten asked, peering out over the valley and seeing nothing.

"Don't be embarrassing, Dad," Butch said.

We hurried down the trail, the rain pelting us. It had increased in strength, coming down in heavy droplets. In a couple of places, we had to pick our way around washouts on the trail.

At last, we came to a straightaway cutting along a steep section of slope barren of trees except for lower down, where the slope grew gentler. At the far end, about two hundred yards away, stood the rest of the group, waiting for us.

Angie cupped her hands and shouted, "Hurry up!"

"Does it look like we're standing still?" Quinten asked.

"So you finally see them?" Butch asked.

"I wished I couldn't see her."

We walked along the straightaway, Angie still calling for us to pick up speed, when I heard something above her shouting.

A low rumble, coming from upslope.

I turned, my heart clenching, and saw a rock the size of my dining room table rolling down toward us. As it bounced and tumbled, it broke away smaller stones as well as big chunks of earth. Within seconds, a section of hillside a good fifty yards wide was roaring down at us.

SEVEN

We ran back the way we had come. I think I screamed. In fact, I was sure I screamed. I only hoped I didn't scream words that I should never say in front of my grandson.

I'm not generally a potty mouth. There are times, however, when certain words are called for.

We ran as the roaring of the landslide filled our ears and the ground trembled beneath our feet. Nothing hit us. The roar subsided, the trembling growing still. We slowed, stopped, and turned, panting and wide-eyed.

I let out a gust of relief to see the other half of our group standing well away and unhurt. I let out another gust of relief to see that Quinten had run in the right direction. He stood panting by my side, foggy glasses askew but otherwise fine.

I looked back at the other group. Between us was a wide swath of chewed-up earth, a broad smear of mud and stone.

The trail had vanished.

I cupped my hands and shouted, "Is everyone okay over there?"

"Yes," Ms. Chipper called back.

"Don't shout!" Angie shouted. "You'll cause another avalanche!"

"You're shouting just as loud as they are!" Butch shouted.

"Quiet!" Angie shouted.

"Everyone stop shouting!" I shouted.

"You're shouting too!" Angie shouted.

Ms. Chipper turned and said something to Angie. She said it in a normal tone, so I didn't hear what she told her, but I could guess. The scandalized look on her face was visible even at a distance. The kids all laughed, even her daughter. Especially her daughter. Poor girl. We don't get to choose our family.

Once Angie was out of the way, Ms. Chipper and I resumed our conversation.

"Is there another way out of here?" I asked. The

trail had vanished, replaced by churned-up mud and loose stones. The kids might have gotten over it safely, but I didn't want them to risk it. I doubted Quinten and I could make it across.

"If you go back to the campsite and continue on the trail another half mile, it branches. Take the upper branch. It angles around this side of Widow's Peak then follows the top of the valley edge before coming down to meet the main trail a couple of miles down the valley."

"How many miles is that going to add to our trip?"

Ms. Chipper studied her map. "About five, with a big gain in altitude. And you'll still need to walk out of the rest of the valley."

I sighed and looked around. The rain had not let up. The air had turned cold and clammy. But we were all dry, and we had a bit of food with us. The kids would be all right. Quinten looked a bit tired, and I certainly felt tired.

I didn't see another option, though.

"We'll do it," I called back to her and then said something I had never said in all my days as a CIA agent. "If all goes well, we'll be at the parking lot a couple of hours before sunset."

If all goes well.

We never said that when planning a mission. Some agents thought it brought bad luck. I had never been superstitious like that, but I avoided saying it because it was a dumb thing to say. Missions never went all well. Something always messed up. A bad guy got away or an agent got hurt or even killed. So I'd never used "if all goes well."

I said it to make the kids feel better. I also said it, if truth be told, to make myself feel better.

My CIA discipline took over and forbade me from thinking of all the things that could go wrong. It only allowed me to think of the potential dangers so I could protect myself against them.

The primary one was the chance that the murderer had not fled after killing Thomas and might still be up here. We had to pass right by the crime scene again. What if he had been waiting for us all to leave and had gone back to clean up the scene? What if he had been watching and had seen me take evidence? He'd want to stop us from taking that to the police.

Martin suggested an even more sinister possibility.

"Do you think the guy who killed Mr. Cardiff started that avalanche to kill us?"

"Ohmigod!" Butch cried. "That's totally what

happened. He tried to crush us and wipe us right off the hillside!"

I glanced at Quinten. His face looked grim. I looked back at Martin and Butch, my too-cool-for-you grandson and the rising star of the football team, and saw two frightened children.

It would have been nice to reassure them, tell them that with such a steep slope and heavy rainfall, it was perfectly natural that there would be a landslide.

But that would be doing them a disservice.

"It might have been."

Their eyes widened. They were accustomed to adults telling them sweet lies. In normal suburban life, that might have been all right, but this was survival.

"If it was him, he would have stuck around to see if we had gotten killed. He'll know we're still alive and might try to hurt us again. Or he might not. We haven't seen him, and he might not want to get close enough for his face to be seen. If we stick together, stay alert, and walk fast, we can probably avoid him."

"If he's up there, then he's on the trail we need to use," Quinten said.

I took a deep breath. "Yes."

"And he probably heard Ms. Chipper giving you directions."

Trust a librarian to get to the facts. "Yes."

I turned back to Ms. Chipper and called, "Is there any other trail out of here?"

"Not one that will get you out today or even tomorrow."

That decided it. I didn't want to spend the night out here with the killer, and we didn't have enough food for an overnight. Water would be no problem; there was an abundance of that at the moment, and I had packed some iodine pills. We could purify water from one of the streams.

"You folks go on ahead," I told her. "The quicker you get out the better. Leave us some food at where the trails meet."

"All right. Good luck!"

Ms. Chipper tried to say that in her usual chipper voice. It did not come off as convincing.

"Let's go," I said, turning back to the others. I found Quinten and Butch had pulled out Swiss Army knives. They looked brand new—a father-and-son set probably purchased for this occasion. Martin had picked up a big stick.

I said nothing. Someone who had set off into the wilderness to kill a man while he was with a group of people would probably laugh at such feeble weapons. I wondered if he had a gun. He hadn't used it, most likely because he'd wanted to kill Thomas Cardiff quietly and perhaps wanted the killing to be up close and personal.

I decided not to tell the others this. If it made them feel better to carry a stick or a little three-inch blade, let them.

As a matter of fact...

I pulled off my pack, reached into it, and took out a survival knife with a nine-inch blade, serrated on the back side and with a compass on the pommel and a hollow hilt that contained a length of extra-strong twine, a tinder box, a couple of iodine pills to purify water, and a needle and thread.

"Whoa," Martin said. "Where did you get that, Grandma?"

The CIA. "Oh, I picked it up many years ago. Your grandfather had one just like it. I'll give it to you when we get back home."

This offer of a gift cheered him up a little.

"They're leaving," Butch said, his usual husky voice coming out soft and quiet.

I turned and saw the others walking down the trail. One by one, they rounded a corner and slipped out of sight. A girl stopped at the back. Melanie.

She waved. Martin raised his stick and shook it over his head like some primitive warrior. Then she, too, rounded the corner and was gone.

"Let's go," I said.

No one said anything as we trudged back to our original campsite, forlorn and abandoned. Thomas's tent was being battered by the rain, its former occupant lying dead not five minutes' walk up the slope. The campfire was cold and black, still sheltered from the rain by the tarp we had not had time to remove.

"Martin, Butch, climb up those trees and fetch the tarp."

"We're going to be out of here before dark," Butch said. "We don't need to make another campfire."

"Just in case. When you get it down, roll it up and secure it to the top of your pack, Butch. You're the strongest."

Without another word, they did as they were told. I kept glancing up at the mineshaft entrance, which I could barely see as a thinning in the greenery. Was he up there somewhere? If he had hurried, he might have paralleled us along the ridge then cut straight down the slope. He might be at the murder scene right now, watching us through the foliage.

It occurred to me that the killer must know this

area very well and knew precisely what paths we would take and where we would camp. He had probably scouted out this region extensively beforehand and knew his intended victim would be coming with the group.

This man was strong, accustomed to life in the wilderness, and knew the area better than we did. He had all the advantages. Even our numbers weren't an advantage—one strong, well-prepared man against a half-blind man, two frightened fourteen-year-olds, and a woman in her seventies.

I gripped my survival knife a little tighter.

I might have been a little old lady, but I was a little old lady with survival and combat training. I was a little old lady who had been through a lot worse than this and come out on top.

Now it looked like I'd have to do it again.

EIGHT

We found the trail just where Ms. Chipper had said it would be, half a mile beyond the camp. One branch continued straight, while the other took a sharp angle up the slope.

I glanced around, nerves taut. The foliage grew thick here, with numerous thick trees and outcroppings of rock. There were plenty of places for an attacker to hide. If I had been with a group of fellow agents, I would have gone off trail, sent out scouts to the front, flanks, and rear, and moved slowly and carefully every step of the way.

But I was not with fellow agents. None of us had a gun, and only I had any training. We had to walk along the narrow trail single file, like a bunch of ducks in a shooting gallery.

Was I doing the right thing? Perhaps it would be best to get off the trail and hide somewhere a few miles away.

That might end up getting us in worse trouble. If we stuck to the trail, we would not get lost, and we might even come across someone who could help, like other hikers or a park ranger. We had seen a couple of hikers heading out of the park on our first day. Today, however, we hadn't seen a soul.

Also, if we moved into the bush and tried to find a place to hide, we'd be out of sight of any potential witnesses if the killer came for us.

Would he try to kill us? Maybe that landslide had been an unhappy coincidence and the killer was really long gone.

Maybe.

I thought about his actions. While he (or she or they, I reminded myself) had kept hidden from view, he had also signaled his presence. That blaze from our first night had been set so that we would see it, and the killer or killers knew that it would send a clear signal to Thomas. It sure had spooked him.

And had the killer deliberately revealed himself by following on the trail at a distance? Had he wanted Thomas, who had remained at the rear of the group for the entire hike, to spot him?

That seemed to entail too great a risk. If the killer knew so much about Thomas and our trip, he would surely know that Thomas would have brought along a high-quality camera with a zoom lens. I was betting Thomas had taken some pictures of the killer, and that was why the killer had risked coming into camp to fetch the camera.

And then there were the words my grandson and his gal had heard Thomas say. He had been muttering about going and confronting someone. Had there been another signal, one that we hadn't seen since we had all been in our tents?

"Martin, did you see anything unusual last night when you were, um, visiting Melanie?" He was right behind me. I was in the lead, and behind him came Butch and then Quinten.

"Like what?"

"Like anything."

Martin thought for a moment. "Well, when I first got up to go over to her tent, I thought I heard some rustling in the bushes. I figured it was a deer, maybe, like the one we saw the first day. Or maybe one of the other kids moving around."

"What direction was this coming from?"

"Uphill, kinda close to camp. I didn't really think anything of it." Martin's face grew serious.

"Do you think it was... the guy that's out there now?"

"Perhaps."

I saw everyone grip their makeshift weapons a little tighter.

"What can you tell me about Mr. Cardiff?"

"He runs the photo lab," Butch said. "That's the only class he teaches. He's also the sub."

"What classes does he substitute for?"

"Whatever," Butch said with a shrug.

Cheerville High was a big school with a lot of classes.

"So he's usually at the school all day?"

"Yeah, I guess."

"What kind of reputation does he have at the school?"

"He's a grouch," Martin said.

"Totally," Butch agreed.

"Why do you say that?"

Martin shrugged. "I don't know. I mean, he's never mean to us or anything, but he's always, like, stressed out over everything. Like once last week, the school forgot to order an update to some photo software, and he got all pissed off."

"Does he ever say or do anything inappropriate?" I asked gently.

Martin looked confused for a moment. "Inappropriate? You mean, like... ew, no!"

I looked at Butch, who also shook his head. It seemed that Thomas really did keep his sleaziness out of school. That relieved me on more than one level. The kids had been safe, and I was investigating the murder of a victim who deserved justice.

"Any other strange behavior?" I asked.

Butch grinned. "Like Boozy Bradford? No."

"I did have one odd experience with him," Quinten said.

"Did he get inappropriate with you, Dad?" Butch asked. He and Martin snickered.

The resilience of youth never ceased to amaze me. Here we were on the run from a killer, and these kids were making jokes about their murdered photography teacher. It reminded me of some of the graveyard humor the Special Forces got into, all of it unprintable.

Quinten blushed. "No, don't be ridiculous. He came into the library to do some research last month. I recognized him from the big parent-teacher meeting we have at the beginning of every school year."

"What was he researching?" I asked.

The trail was getting steeper, and I had to watch

my footing more than the forest around me. I didn't like that. Not at all.

"He wanted to see the microfilm for newspapers in the region. Not the Cheerville paper but the ones for all the surrounding towns."

"Microfilm? Was he looking at old papers?"

"No, he wanted editions from the last five years. He got irritated when I told him we don't have them for those years. Everything's online now, and with our limited budget, we don't order newspaper microfilm anymore."

"So what did he do then?"

"He used one of our public computers."

That was interesting. As a photojournalist, he would have known the articles were available online. Most people knew that even without a background in newspaper work. It could only mean that he didn't want to access them from his own computer. He was being so careful, in fact, that he didn't even want to use a public computer except as a last resort.

"Did you see what he was looking at?"

"No. I had other work to do. I did notice one odd thing though. When I passed by him to reshelve some books, he popped up another window."

"Ooooh." Butch got a knowing look. "He was looking at porn."

To my surprise, Quinten didn't scold his son. "That's what I assumed. It's happened before. Now I'm not so sure that's what he was doing."

"Do you remember him doing anything else?" I asked.

"Wow, Grandma. You're acting like a detective," Martin said.

"I think that's a good idea at the moment, don't you?"

"Just keep your clothes on," Martin said with a chuckle.

The other two gave him a very odd look. Quinten did what many people do in awkward situations—he ignored the comment entirely.

"He sat at the computer for an hour or so, taking notes, and then he went to look at the law books we have in back and took another hour or so on those. Took a bunch more notes there too."

"I don't suppose you saw any of these notes."

"No. Sorry. We don't pry into the patrons' research."

Normally I appreciated that trait in librarians. Now I felt as if we might have missed something vital.

We continued up the slope, hearing only the steady patter of rain. The trail made several switchbacks, and I felt myself beginning to tire. Even though it was still well before noon, my legs had that heavy feeling you get at the end of a long day of marching.

I bit my lip and tried to ignore it. I had done pretty well for the first two days. It appeared that three days was my limit.

Well, I didn't have the luxury of limits, not right now. We kept going.

"Look," Martin said when we were nearly to the top of the ridge.

I turned to where he was pointing and saw a mineshaft about two hundred yards to the right of the trail. Because of the roughness of the terrain, it had not been visible until just now, and walking another few steps would have put it out of sight again.

What had caught my grandson's attention was not the mine itself—we had passed two or three already that day—but the fact that a couple of the boards had been removed from the entrance, allowing a narrow space that a person might pass through.

We stopped. The boards lay at the entrance, as if they had fallen off naturally. I wondered.

"Should we check it out?" Butch asked.

"Check what out?" Quinten asked.

I did not relish the idea of exploring that mine. But it seemed too important to ignore.

"Let's take a look. Kids, you stay here."

Quinten and I cut along the slope toward the mine entrance. The two boys followed about twenty yards behind us. They obviously didn't want to be left alone on the trail. I couldn't blame them, although I did motion for them to hang back a bit more.

As we approached the entrance, I saw my suspicions were correct. While the rain had erased any footprints, I could see the grass had been trampled down in front as if someone had been walking around there frequently. I also noticed that the two boards, while positioned to look as if they had simply fallen off the barrier, had been placed with the nails down. If they had naturally fallen off, the nails would have been pointing up. Our friend obviously didn't want to risk stepping on a nail, and so he had flipped them, thinking no one would get close enough to notice.

We paused. Quinten and I exchanged a glance, and the librarian nodded.

Brave folks, librarians. They fight for the right to information, for people to read whatever they want to read, and for their privacy to read whatever they like without the government looking over their shoulder. I'd never fought alongside a librarian, however. That was a different type of bravery. I wondered if Quinten had that sort of bravery too.

Hopefully, I wouldn't have to find out.

Quinten moved toward the mine. I held him back and motioned for us to circle around it so that if someone was standing right inside the entrance, he couldn't strike at us. Of course, if he had a gun, he could shoot us, but if he had a gun, we were all going to die anyway.

We edged around the entrance and peered in. Daylight filtered inside just enough that we could see that it had been occupied. The rubble had been cleared out from the front part of the mineshaft and lay in a heap about ten feet back. Among the rocks and sticks were a couple of cans of Sterno that looked new, the blue labels unfaded. There were also a couple of plastic wrappers from camp meals, the ready-made kind that you only need to add water to and heat over a stove. Quinten flicked on a flashlight, and we saw the gleam of a couple empty water bottles farther in.

"Ms. Chipper would get angry if she saw all this litter," Quinten said.

I examined the wooden props holding up the walls and ceiling. They looked newer and better made than the others I'd seen.

"I think this mine is from the late period of prospecting, back in the 1940s, rather than the turn of the century or earlier," I said.

"How do you know that?" Quinten asked.

"Didn't you hear Ms. Chipper's lecture on the first day?"

"No. Butch was making fart noises."

"It should be stable enough. Our suspect obviously thought so. Let's go in and take a closer look."

"Is he in there?" Martin's concerned voice asked.

"No, but he was," I replied.

The boys hurried to join us.

"Keep watch outside," I told them. "We're going to investigate his campsite."

The opening was a slantwise hole in the latticework of moldy boards that was low enough that even I had to duck to enter. I felt a twinge in my back as I did so.

Not now, I told my body. *Mr. Chong and his needles are miles away.*

Quinten joined me. For a moment, we stood side by side, peering down the mineshaft with our flashlights.

The floor, covered with dust and a scattering of dirt, showed a confusing blur of marks. I supposed they were from the sleeping bag and other gear being set down and moved around. Near the back, close to the heap of rocks and twigs that the occupant had swept out, were a couple of muddy footprints that hadn't been obscured.

I pulled out my strings to measure them.

"Why are you bending over so slowly?" Quinten asked. "Do you have a bad back?"

"Yes," I admitted. "It comes and goes."

"Let me do it."

"Chivalry isn't dead."

"I'm a member of the Knights of the Round Bookshelf."

"Just measure the footprints."

He compared the string lengths to the dimensions of the boot prints and got an exact match.

I felt my skin prickle.

So he had camped here, out of the rain, cooking his food on the Sterno stove right inside the entrance, where it would be well ventilated but the dim glow could not be seen except for along a short length of the trail, a trail nobody would be hiking on at night. More importantly, we wouldn't be on that trail, since it wasn't part of the planned hike. The mine was close enough to our campsite that he could get there easily and then retreat here, and it was stable enough that he could camp here safely.

He had known our movements, and he knew the terrain like the back of his hand. It seemed he had all the advantages.

"Psst, Grandma," Martin said in a frightened whisper. I turned to find both boys right up against the wood barrier, looking terrified.

"What?"

"There's somebody moving around out here."

NINE

I ducked back out through the space in the boards, feeling another twinge.

"Where?" I asked, my voice coming out strained.

Butch pointed. "Down there, by that clump of trees." The boy indicated a cluster of trees about halfway down the valley, a good quarter of a mile away.

I stared but saw nothing. "You sure?" I asked.

"Yeah," Martin said. "We both saw it."

"It could be someone on the lower branch of the trail," I said. "Perhaps another hiker."

"Or it could be him, Grandma. Let's get out of here."

"Hey!" Quinten said from inside the mine. "I found something."

"What?" I asked, sticking my head through a small gap in the boards. I did not want to have to duck through the entrance again if I could help it. My back was still complaining about the last time.

"I found a receipt." He held up a crumpled piece of paper.

"You have sharp eyes." First time for everything.

"I cleaned my glasses."

"Grandma! I saw him again!"

I pulled my head out of the gap and turned. "Where?"

"Down there in the same place."

"He was looking at us," Butch said.

"We need to get out of here!" Martin said.

Quinten came out of the mineshaft and grabbed his pack. By the time he had put it on, his glasses had fogged again. I picked up my pack as well, keeping an eye on the clump of trees. As I turned my torso to put my arms through the straps, I felt a sharp twinge.

Not now!

"I don't see him," I said through gritted teeth.

"I swear to God he was there," Martin said.

"I saw him too," Butch said. Both looked terrified.

"Let's go," I said. "He's pretty far down the slope.

If we keep a good pace, he won't be able to keep up with us."

Quinten gave me a knowing look. He, too, had figured out that whoever this was, he was fit and knowledgeable about the area. He could catch up with us if he wanted to.

"The top of the ridge is open and more exposed," I said. "He won't be able to sneak up on us there. Once we get into the clear, we'll take a look at what you found."

Quinten nodded, and without another word, we headed out.

Marching quickly up the steep switchbacks really began to take a toll on my legs. Where they had felt heavy before, now they began to feel sore as the lactic acid built up in my overused muscles. I soldiered on, glancing over my shoulder every few moments, hoping to catch any sign of movement downhill from us.

I saw nothing. Whoever was down there was being careful.

I would have liked to think that perhaps the boys had seen another hiker, someone innocent going along the path. I couldn't quite convince myself. The worst-case scenario was always the best one to plan for.

We passed the last of the trees and came to the rocky upper reaches of the valley, where only a few shrubs and clumps of grass grew.

"Everyone, hunch over as you walk," I instructed.

"Why?" Martin asked.

I took a deep breath, preparing to steal a bit of my grandson's innocence. "To make less of a target in case he has a gun."

That got no reply. In fact, no one said a thing for a long time. I couldn't bear to look at Martin. I didn't want to see his face.

Walking hunched over began to make my back twinge. I felt tempted to stand back upright but was afraid that would set a bad example for the boys and they would straighten up, too, making better targets.

No shots came.

We made it to the top of the ridge just as my calves started screaming. The ridgetop was fairly flat and a good hundred yards wide, with a few bushes and several outcroppings of rock. The trail ran along its center, putting us out of sight of the trail leading up. We were all grateful we could stand up straight again, although it worried me that we couldn't see if our hidden friend was coming up after us.

The ridgetop gave us a spectacular view. While

we couldn't see the closest part of the slope, we got a sweeping vista of the valley and the other ridges, valleys, hills, and mountains all around. Not a soul was in sight, nor was any sign of civilization. It would have been beautiful if we hadn't been in mortal danger.

And the landscape itself was a danger. With such rough terrain and no map, I could see how easily we could get lost here. Our path down the valley was clear enough, but if we got off it, we'd be in trouble.

Our pursuer knew this, of course.

My back twinged again. My legs felt like lead. "Let's stop a minute," I said, leaning against a boulder.

"Grandma, we need to keep going!"

Peru, 1980: I'm hustling the mayor of a rural village over the foothills of the Andes as we're being pursued by guerrillas of the Sendero Luminoso, the "Shining Path." Their shining path is supposed to lead to communism for Peru and, eventually, all of Latin America. They say they want to free the peasants from the chains of capitalist oppression, and they'll strangle or stone to death any peasant who doesn't obey them.

Some liberation.

Guzman Alvarez, mayor of Dos Colinas, population four hundred, is one of those brave peasants who has stood up to the rebels. That got his brother killed and him nearly so when they attacked his house.

Now I'm trying to get him to a Peruvian army base and safety.

I've gotten separated from the rest of the CIA team and the other peasants we're trying to save. Guzman and I are alone, struggling through thick bush and over steep hills. Guzman is of peasant stock, born to these hills, and normally would be outpacing the little gun-toting gringa who has come to save him.

Bullet wounds through his shoulder and thigh are slowing him down.

"No puedo, Barbara," he gasps, blood staining the field dressings I've put on him. "I can't."

"Just a little farther," I say.

"Let's stop a minute," he says, leaning against a boulder.

"Guzman, we need to keep going!"

A shot rings out from the jungle. Guzman falls dead.

"You're right, Martin. Let's go."

We walked a mile along the ridge top, glancing back every now and then. At points, we could see several hundred yards behind us, but we caught no glimpse of our pursuer.

It appeared he wasn't following us.

That worried me. It meant he was going by a different route, a route we didn't know. He could end up ahead of us.

We came to a cluster of rocks with a good view of the path both ahead and behind. Here, I called a rest. My muscles were begging me to stop, and we still hadn't looked at that receipt Quinten had found in the mine. Fear had momentarily overcome our curiosity.

We took off our packs and sat for several minutes, the boys looking nervously around us. My muscles slowly began to forgive me, although I knew they'd start complaining again as soon as I got up. The rain still pattered down, and other than a slight wind, it was eerily silent.

Quinten took out the receipt and handed it to me. I held it at arm's length, not wanting to rummage through my pack for my reading glasses. Quinten lifted up his rain-fogged glasses and got in close, squinting at it from an inch away.

"Omigod, give it to me," Martin said, snatching it away. He looked at it for a second. "It's from Footloose Outdoors Supplies in Millersburg."

Millersburg was about twenty miles from Cheerville. Another sleepy bedroom district.

"Whoa," Butch said. "That's where we got our tents."

"Dad and I bought my tent there too," Martin said. "He told me it was the only big hiking store around."

I nodded. I'd heard that, too, although I had gone to Megaton Army Surplus. Old habits die hard.

"So I guess it's not surprising that the killer went there for his gear," Quinten said. "What's on the receipt?"

Martin read through it. "Four cans of Sterno, ten Insta Cook Camp Meals, and twenty Power Up Protein Bars."

"My God, we're dealing with a psychopath," I said. "No sane person would ever eat that many protein bars. What's the date?"

"A month ago."

Long enough that the clerk would probably not remember the killer but recently enough that the hike's itinerary had already been sent to faculty and parents.

"Was it paid by cash or credit card?" I asked.

"Cash."

Of course it was. Our killer had been careful.

Not too careful. He could have just as easily gone into the city to buy his supplies and avoided suspicion.

Or perhaps not. He was obviously a seasoned hiker and familiar with the local state park. Thus he was probably a regular at the Millersburg shop. Not going there the previous month might have attracted as much attention as going there.

I took the receipt and stowed it safely in an inner pocket in my raincoat. This was a vital piece of evidence. A good detective could track down the killer this way. Of course, a defense attorney would say there was no proof that the person camping in the mine was the same person who killed Thomas Cardiff, but it was certainly a big step closer to breaking open the case, another piece of the puzzle that would lead to a picture of what had happened.

Now all I had to do was get out of the state park alive and hand it over to the police.

I checked my watch. It was a little past noon. Plenty of time to get out of the park. The worst part of the hike was over. All we had to do was follow the ridge a short way then go downhill to our original trail, where a food cache would be waiting courtesy of Ms. Chipper. From there, it was mostly downhill except for one low ridge we had to cross over. We could be back in the parking lot well before dark. With any luck, we'd meet the police on the way up.

Of course, the killer knew this too. He also knew that we had been to his campsite. Even though he would be unaware that he had left an incriminating receipt among his rubbish, he'd want to stop us.

I popped a couple of painkillers and washed them down with a drink of water from my canteen.

"Let's keep moving," I said.

My back twinged in protest as I put on my pack, and my legs felt heavy and sluggish. I ignored the signals my body was giving me. I didn't have time for them.

Not far beyond the cluster of rocks, we came to a spot where the trail bent around a patch of rough terrain and took us close to the edge of the ridge. It turned out to be directly above where the landslide had occurred. The slope was curved inward to form a broad funnel, and a little way down, we could see where the landslide had started. A hole in the earth like the gum after a tooth has been extracted showed where a boulder had been dislodged. With the rain and erosion, the entire slope had been weakened, and that boulder bouncing downhill had set off the landslide.

The killer must have pried that boulder loose

with a crowbar or something in an attempt to kill us or at least block our path so as to kill us later.

The boulder had been a sizeable one. It would have taken some serious strength to pry it loose, and when it had fallen, it could have dislodged enough earth to take the killer with it.

He had risked his life to try and kill a group of innocent schoolchildren.

"He's a total psycho," Butch whispered.

I nodded, and we continued.

We got to the downward trail within a matter of minutes and began to descend into the forested level of the valley. That got me nervous. The trees and underbrush offered too many places to hide.

"Everyone keep watch," I said.

"Okay," Quinten replied, stumbling over a root.

I sighed, reminding myself that I had been in worse situations than this.

I glanced at Martin. Sure, I had been in worse situations. Plenty of times. Except the personal stakes had never been so high.

Descending put new strains on my body. The slippery footing and steep angle added pressure to the back of my legs and, by extension, the small of my back, where Mr. Chong had been sticking his needles.

Now it felt like a dagger had gotten stuck in there.

I thought through the contents of my pack, wondering what I could get rid of, and realized there was quite a lot.

Stopping, I took off the pack and cast aside the tent, ground sheet, sleeping bag, toiletries, a paperback, and a spare set of clothes. I kept the dirty socks in case the ones I had on got wet.

"You want me to carry your pack, Grandma?" Martin asked.

"No, I'm fine now." I was still tired, but at least my back didn't twinge anymore.

It might later.

I realized that three days had become my limit for what I used to call "baby hikes." If we had kept to the itinerary, with no extra ridge to climb or a mine to explore, I thought I would have been fine. Worn out but not in pain.

After I lightened my load, it was a quick descent to where the two trails met.

"There it is!" Martin cried, pointing to a white plastic supermarket bag sitting at the connection of the two trails.

That lifted my spirits. "Let's see what food Ms. Chipper left us. I could do with a snack."

My spirits dampened as we drew closer. The bag didn't look very full.

After another few steps, I realized why.

It lay flat on the ground, weighed down by a fist-sized stone, and appeared to be completely empty. One corner flapped forlornly in the breeze.

Our pursuer had gotten here before us.

TEN

We all realized the same thing at around the same time, except for Quinten, who had to be told.

"It's a trap," he said, trying to peer through his foggy glasses. "We should go another way."

"What other way?" Martin asked.

"If he wanted to make a trap, he would have left the food in the bag, not warned us he had been here," I said.

"He's playing with us," Butch said. He moved closer to his dad. Even though he was nearly a head taller than the librarian, he still looked to him for support. Martin moved closer to me too.

Gripping my survival knife, I moved to the bag, looking carefully around me.

The bag was, indeed, empty. A note written in

ballpoint pen was wedged below the rock. Although the paper was soggy from the rain, the writing remained legible, and it was in large enough letters that I didn't have to embarrass myself in front of my grandson again.

Barbara, Quinten, Martin, and Butch,

We've left you a big bundle of snacks and the map. I know my way around, so I don't need it. You shouldn't need it either if you keep on the same path we came up, but I'm leaving it just in case you have to avoid whoever killed poor Thomas. We're going to the parking lot as quick as we can. We'll send help. Be careful, and good luck!

Marjory Chipper

He had taken the map. The only reason to do that is if he wanted to scare us off the trail and get us lost. Then he could hunt us down at leisure, and the police wouldn't know where to find us.

Much as I didn't want to, I told the others what I thought. Quinten looked grim but not surprised, as if he had figured it out already. Butch's eyes welled with tears, and his lip trembled. Martin slumped and looked at the ground.

"Look, it's not as bad as it seems," I told them. "He obviously doesn't have a gun, or he would have shot us by now. Plus, we're four against one." That got me some measuring looks. "It's only a few hours to the parking lot, and we might even bump into some other hikers."

"No one's going to be hiking in this weather," Martin grumbled.

"Maybe, maybe not. You never know. People might have gone farther into the state park and are now leaving because the weather turned bad. Or maybe Ms. Chipper found a park ranger and told him what happened. We could bump into some help at any moment."

Martin looked at me. "We haven't seen anyone all day, and if we do bump into someone, how do we know it isn't that creep?"

Good point.

"Well, if that creep does come around, we'll be ready for him."

I shucked off my backpack, went over to a tree, and used my knife to cut off a straight branch that was about half an inch thick. Quickly, I used the blade to strip off the little twigs and all the bark until I was left with a straight shaft.

"You making a walking stick?" Quinten asked.

"No. Don't mind me. Keep watching the woods around us."

I cut off the front end and sharpened the back

end. I then pulled out the string from the hollow handle of my pocket knife and lashed the knife onto the flat end.

I now had a five-foot-long spear with a spiked butt. Good for stabbing and even jabbing backward if someone came up behind me and I didn't have time to turn around.

"That's epic!" Martin said. "Can you make me one?"

"You don't have a knife."

"At least sharpen my stick," he said, waving the crude club he had been carrying all this time.

"We need to get going, Martin."

The truth was, I was afraid he'd stab the wrong person with it. Me, for example.

"Where did you learn how to do that?" he asked.

"When I was younger, I did a lot of hiking." True enough, if you counted wilderness counterinsurgency warfare as "hiking."

I kept a sharp eye all around us, especially uphill, in case our friend decided to start another landslide. Luckily, on this part of the trail, the slope was gentler, with more trees that spoke of a thicker layer of topsoil. This was not a good place to try such a nasty surprise.

Unfortunately, the slope did not stay that way.

Up ahead, I could see another steep, bare patch of the ridge almost identical to the one where the killer had laid the last trap. We stopped and stared, saying nothing. A trail branched off the one we walked on, making several switchbacks as it went downhill to the river below. We decided not to make ourselves targets and took the lower path.

The trail down to the valley bottom was grueling. Even with my lightened pack, my back and legs were aching by the time we made it to the bottom.

What we saw there made me forget all about my pain for a moment.

The small creek we had glimpsed from time to time from the trail had swollen with the rain and become a wide stream. The trail led right up to the water's edge then continued on the other side. I imagined that there had been a set of easy stepping stones for hikers to cross, but they were now totally submerged.

Going right up to the water, I stuck my spear down as far as I could reach. It almost disappeared before I touched bottom.

"The stream is a good four feet deep, and considering how fast it's going, it could sweep us right along if we tried to wade across it."

"Plus, if we get wet in this temperature, we might

get hypothermia," Quinten said, sneezing as if to add emphasis to his words.

"We can go along the river on this side," Butch suggested. "All we have to do is follow it until that ridge comes into view. What was it called, Miner's Ridge? Then we climb that and find the trail again."

"That's just what he wants us to do," I said.

"Then what else can we do?" Martin cried, throwing his hands in the air. "We can't cross the river, we can't go back the way we came, we can't go across that exposed part without getting crushed, we…"

I put a reassuring hand on his shoulder. "Let me think."

It was true that we couldn't cross the river, but could we go back the way we had come? I tried to anticipate our adversary's next move. He surely knew the creek had swollen with the heavy rains, and he knew that by setting off that landslide, he'd frighten us away from taking the direct path.

He had sent us down here, right where he wanted us. Our next obvious move was to do just what Butch had suggested: skirt the river to get to Miner's Ridge and climb over it to link up with the trail again.

Somewhere in the thick woods between us and

that trail, he'd pounce. If he could kill all of us—certainly a strong possibility—then he could dump us all in the river. Our bodies might not be found for days or even weeks.

So if he was coming down, the smartest thing for us to do was to go up, all the way back to the top of the ridge. With a bit of luck, he wouldn't spot us, and we could follow the ridge out of the park.

I peered through the trees to the top of the ridge far, far above. My heart fell. There was no way I could make it all the way back up. I'd start slowing everybody down right from the start as we climbed this damp, slippery slope, and I'd be exhausted by the time we got up the side of the valley, assuming I'd make it at all. After that, we'd be exposed on the valley top, with me most likely not able to continue.

Of course, I could make them leave me, but that was Horror Movie Thinking, as Martin would say, and would put us in an even worse position than we already were in.

"We'll go up Miner's Ridge," I said at last, "but we won't go on the route he's expecting us to. Once we get up the ridge, we'll try and find a way to dodge him."

"But, Grandma, he'll be waiting for us."

"This forest is large and dense. He can't see far.

He'll wait for us somewhere obvious, like on the trail."

"Or on top of the ridge," Martin said. "He could be up there right now."

"Not yet. He had to set the landslide from above. He's got a long climb to get down, and then if he wants to get us onto the top of Miner's Ridge, he'll have to cut through rough country to make it. That buys us time."

"Then we better hurry up," Quinten said.

We set out, following the side of the stream. It proved to be rough going, walking along the slick slope through woods and underbrush, occasionally having to clamber over outcroppings of rock. I could already feel myself tiring.

At least the forest canopy sheltered us from the worst of the rain. Instead of getting struck with a constant rainfall, we got pattered with occasional drops that made it through the leaves or dripped off the foliage. The forest floor was soaked, however, and the going was uneven and slippery.

Then it happened. A step over a log, a rabbit hole, or something hidden under a carpet of leaves, and my ankle twisted. I stumbled, using the butt end of my spear to steady myself. A brief pain in my ankle, followed by a much sharper jab in my back.

I hissed through clenched teeth and hugged a tree, slowly flexing my injured leg. Ignoring the worried questions of my companions, I slowly turned my ankle. Just a bad twist. It would be fine in a minute or two.

My back, on the other hand, was messed up good and proper. I felt tension clamp down on the lower portion, sending stiffness and pain up the length of my spine.

"Help me get my pack off," I groaned.

Someone did. I couldn't even see who, not daring to turn my head in case it added to the pain.

"Side pocket—there's an aspirin bottle."

"You look like you need something stronger," Quinten said, pulling out the bottle.

"I don't have anything stronger."

When I had first developed my bad back, my doctor had given me a prescription for a popular brand of opioid painkillers, an entire month's worth of a strong dose with a chance to renew the prescription every month after that.

I had refused. It was a trap. Having spent many years fighting the drug war overseas, I knew enough about the chemistry of the stuff to know not to fall into taking it. Even someone who doesn't like drugs and doesn't have an addictive personality will become addicted after taking a regular dose of opioids for a certain length of time. It changes the body's chemistry, creating a physical addiction. Willpower and self-discipline are worth nothing; your own body betrays you. Once addicted, it is extremely difficult to wean oneself off it. I was appalled that my physician, who certainly knew this as well as I did, would give me such a prescription. I was even more appalled that it was common practice.

So instead, I gobbled aspirin like some aspirin junkie, drinking a long guzzle of water and eating some of my small supply of nuts to keep my stomach settled.

I forced myself to relax, trying to will my back into not feeling pain. The aspirin would take some time to kick in, time we did not have. Even now, the man who was hunting us was scurrying down the side of the valley, looking for a good ambush spot.

"We need to get moving."

Martin tossed aside my pack. "We can ditch this."

"What about my things?"

"They're already in our packs," Quinten said.

I'd been so involved in my own discomfort that I

hadn't noticed them divvying up my possessions among themselves. Bless them.

Lebanon, 1981.

Five fellow operatives and I are sneaking through the rough mountains on the border between Lebanon and Syria. We are being chased by a splinter group of radical Islamic terrorists who think the more mainstream terror groups are too soft. They want to kill more people quicker, and that's what they set out to do, at least until we took out their main bombmaker. The region's school buses are safe again.

We are not. The Islamists have figured out who took out their man and have tracked us. They're only a mile or so behind us: two dozen heavily armed fighters who aren't afraid to die, searching for us.

The night is moonless, but the rocky hills are all but barren of vegetation. There is nowhere to hide. Only distance and darkness will keep us from getting killed.

And I know they're gaining on us. Two of our team are wounded, including myself. I've taken a flesh wound in the thigh that makes every step an agony. The other operative took a gut shot and lies groaning on a makeshift stretcher carried by my husband, James, and another man. They're strong, the wounded man is light, and they are making good time.

I am not.

I'm using my M16 as a crutch and hobbling over the rocky hills at a slower and slower rate.

The terrorists are no doubt moving much faster, scouring the hills in a search that will inevitably lead them to find us.

We all know it, and yet I cannot go any faster.

Not until James hands his end of the stretcher to a female operative and comes back to me.

"I can't—"

I don't get to finish my sentence. Without a word, he pulls out a small photograph from his pocket and shoves it in my face. Although it is too dark to see, I know what it is.

A photo of Frederick, our chubby little toddler, playing happily in my parents' home.

"Move."

That's all James says before he goes back to help carry the stretcher.

That's all he needs to say.

I find the strength within me to carry on, and we get away, out of Lebanon, out of the mission, and back home.

Home to my son.

Right now, that same son, grown from a chubby toddler to a chubby adult, was waiting unaware at home, thinking he would see his own son and his mother in a few hours.

"Let's go," I said, using my homemade spear as a crutch as I walked at a normal rate through the woods. The others, surprised at my sudden move, hurried to join me.

I was still in pain. I still had limited movement, but I was not going to let that stop me from getting my grandson safely back to Frederick and Alicia.

ELEVEN

To keep my mind off the agony of my back, I began to grill Quinten and the boys, hoping to find some more clues to the identity of the man hunting us.

"Did Thomas ever come into the library at other times?" I asked Quinten. I could hear how strained my voice sounded. The librarian was courteous enough not to point it out.

"Not that I can recall. That's why I remembered it, because it was so unusual. Several of the teachers are regulars, checking out books to design assignments for the kids or for their own personal reading. Thomas had never come in, or if he had, he certainly wasn't a regular."

"So he wanted to look at something without leaving an Internet trace. He wanted to look at old local newspapers and some legal books and didn't want anyone to know."

"He sure didn't appreciate my presence. I could feel that right off."

"Do you think he recognized you as a parent of one of his students?"

"I don't think so. I'd never met him personally, just saw him introduced on stage at that big parent-teacher meeting."

"Have you ever seen him anywhere else around Cheerville?"

"Not that I can recall."

We must have been getting close to Miller's Ridge. I told everyone to be extra aware of our surroundings. The ground was growing rockier, thinning the trees and reducing the underbrush. That would make us more visible. It would make our enemy more visible too. He was out there somewhere, searching or waiting.

Next, I turned my attention to the boys.

"You mentioned Thomas had a bad temper. Did he ever have arguments with any of the other teachers or staff?"

"No," Butch said. "He was always grumbling about stuff, like the school not ordering things or the state ripping us off."

"Ripping you off?"

"Like, not giving funding and stuff. He always said the politicians didn't give a damn about education."

Actually, he didn't use the word "damn." I was in too much pain and we were all in too much danger for us to care.

"Did he use such language in front of the students?" Quinten asked.

"All the time," Martin said with a chuckle.

"Never when other teachers could hear," Butch said.

"No," Martin agreed.

The ground began to rise, and the stream cut off to our right. The ridge appeared through the trees, a rocky slope dotted with trees and small bushes. Too exposed. I couldn't see where the stream went. I supposed it cut around Miller's Ridge at some point in a hairpin turn and continued down the valley as the larger stream we had seen at the beginning of the hike. I was tempted to continue skirting the stream, but the way looked rough, and I couldn't tell how long it would take. Better to go up and over the ridge.

But he'd be waiting there. I had been hoping we'd find a place to avoid him, some path we could take that he wouldn't expect, but he had corralled us all too well.

I looked around. The only choices were up the ridge in front of us, up the side of the valley all the way to the top—something I couldn't do before and certainly couldn't do now—or cut to the right along Miller's Ridge, scrambling above that swollen creek.

None of those options held much promise.

"Cool," Martin whispered.

"What?" I asked.

"Nothing. It's stupid."

"Tell me."

He gestured at where the creek turned, forming an oval body of water like a swelling in the creek.

"There must be a cave or something that's letting some of the water through. Remember that little waterfall we saw coming up? That's on the other side of the ridge. I don't know why I was thinking about it. I told you it was stupid."

I grabbed him by the shoulder. "Not at all, Martin. You just showed us how to get out of here!"

My grandson blinked. "I did?"

Quinten snapped his fingers. "I get it. If the waterfall we saw is only part of the stream, then the rest of the river goes along a side valley. It's all down-hill, and it will get us out of the park."

"That's right," I said. "And if I remember right, the county road that we took to get here parallels the edge of the state park. I recall I went over a bridge. This stream must go under that bridge. So if we follow it, we'll end up at the county road."

Martin's eyes lit up. "I see. The killer guy is expecting us to go over this ridge."

Butch snickered. "Hump this ridge, like Ms. Chipper said."

"Such a charming young man, aren't you? Indeed, you're right. He's thinking we'll go over the ridge to get back onto the path and is no doubt waiting for us somewhere along there. But we'll trick him by taking another way out of the park, one that's every bit as clear as the path."

Martin's face clouded. "Can you make it, Grandma?"

I studied the steep slope with its loose, wet rocks. My legs were exhausted. My back throbbed. My range of motion was limited.

"I have to."

We set off. Every step was torture, and I could tell I was slowing them down.

I wasn't the only one who was tired. All of us were. The rain pattered down incessantly. Martin's stomach growled. We hadn't eaten anything since breakfast.

"How much food do we have?" I asked. "I have a small bag of raisins and nuts, just a few handfuls, and an orange."

Martin shrugged. "Some gummy bears. That's it."

"I have a two apples and a bag of sesame seeds," Quinten said, "plus a bag of cornmeal I was carrying for Ms. Chipper. We were going to make corn cakes for breakfast this morning."

I shook my head. We'd have to cook that with water, and that meant a fire. That meant signaling where we were.

"I have a couple of power bars," Butch said.

"Pull them out," I said.

We each took half of one and munched them as we walked.

The food situation gave me something else to worry about. Lunchtime had come and gone, and while everyone was too nervous to complain about hunger, the rigorous hike we'd been doing was beginning to tire us, and we still had a long way to walk.

The killer, we could be sure, had plenty of food and energy.

"How's everyone's water supply?" I asked.

Everyone reported that they were almost out.

"It's not hot," Martin said.

"Gotta keep hydrated, man," Butch said. "That's what Coach always tells us."

"You're quite correct," I said, pulling an iodine tablet out of the hilt of my survival knife. "Butch, I saw you had a big plastic bottle for water."

"Yeah. It's empty."

"Put this tablet in it and fill it in the stream. Then shake it up. The iodine will kill any germs."

"It also helps you pass radiation through your system," Quinten said.

"I don't think it's likely the killer is armed with a nuclear weapon," I replied.

"Or pythons," Quinten said with a smile.

"Radioactive pythons," Butch said. He went down to the stream edge and filled the bottle. If he shook it for a minute, the iodine dissolved and turned the water reddish. "No murderer is gonna nuke us!"

Martin gave his friend a thumbs-up. Not for the first time since the murder, I was amazed at how quickly young people could bounce back from trouble. I could tell they were scared and hungry, but they still managed to make jokes.

Once we got started again, Martin said, "Hey,

you know, there might have been a fight between Mr. Cardiff and someone on the staff."

"Really? Who?"

"Orrin. The janitor."

"What's his last name?" I asked.

Martin shrugged. "Just Orrin."

"You call the janitors by their first names?" I didn't like that. Just because they had a humble job didn't mean they didn't deserve respect.

"Yeah. Everybody does."

"So what happened?"

"Nothing I saw. Orrin got fired three weeks ago. Nobody knows why. He seemed cool. Kinda quiet, but he never snapped at us for making a mess like the other janitors do. One day, we were in the photo lab working on stuff, and someone said they hadn't seen Orrin in a while. We all got to wondering what had happened to him, and Mr. Cardiff got this really nasty grin on his face, like a vampire or something."

"More like an evil clown," Butch said.

"Definitely like an evil clown," Martin agreed. "Then he said, 'You're never going to see him around here anymore. That's all been taken care of.' It was pretty weird, like he was bragging he got Orrin fired or something."

"Are you sure this janitor was fired?" I asked.

"Yeah, totally," Butch said. "Someone asked our coach about it, and he said Orrin got canned. He looked really uncomfortable about it and wouldn't say what happened."

"Interesting," I murmured.

"Orrin... Orrin... that name rings a bell," Quinten said to himself. "It's an unusual name. I've heard it somewhere before, though." After a minute, he snapped his fingers. "I know! A woman came in a few months back to do some genealogy. Cathy or Carol or something. Common name. She said she wanted to research her family, so I helped her out. I remember she mentioned her brother's name was Orrin. That stuck with me because it was so unusual."

"Do you remember what the last name was?"

"Yes, because it's one of the older families here in Cheerville. It comes up a lot. The name is Hitt."

I thought of the blazing H we had seen on the hillside that first night and Thomas Cardiff's reaction to it.

"Was this janitor young and well built?" I asked the boys.

"Yeah, he's totally buff," Butch said. "The coach had him help out sometimes. That guy could run and hit like a pro."

"What does he look like?"

"About six foot, short blond hair. Old but not too old, you know? Like maybe thirty."

"That's not old."

"Yeah, like old but not ancient."

Wonderful.

Martin looked at me. "You think he's the murderer? Because of that fire that looked like an H."

"It's certainly a possibility—ow!"

I had twisted my ankle again on the slope, sending a jab of pain up my back. The others gathered around as I leaned against a tree, face contorted in agony.

For a long minute, I stood there, motionless. Then I gingerly tested my ankle. It was a bit sore, but like the last time, I hadn't sprained it. The real problem was my back. Slowly, I took a couple cautious little steps. Each one was torture.

"You okay, Grandma?" Martin asked.

"I'll be fine in a minute," I whispered.

No I won't. I'm not going to make it.

TWELVE

The next mile or so took an excruciatingly long time. I hobbled forward, twisted like some old crone and using my spear as a crutch. I had to watch every step. Another twist like that and I'd be down for the count.

At last, we came to where the end of the ridge sloped down to the river and the water made a tight turn around it. We picked our way carefully around the turn and saw the river flowing down an unfamiliar valley, parallel to the one we had been hiking in all this time.

"We made it," Quinten said with a relieved smile. "He won't look for us here."

"I hope not," I replied, popping more aspirin. "It

would be best if we kept going as quickly as possible."

I checked my watch, and my heart sank. Sunset was in less than three hours. We wouldn't make it to the county road before dark.

It didn't matter. Even in the dark, it would be easy enough to follow the stream and see the road and bridge. I would have to walk with even more care, though. If worse came to worst, I could make them leave me. In the dark, if I were hidden in the forest, the killer would not be able to find me, and they could get to the road and find help.

The late hour was a problem but not a big one.

A much bigger problem came half a mile down the valley.

The side of the valley, already steeper than what we had crossed before, was blocked by an outcropping of rock that formed a ten-foot-high wall in front of us, jutting out into the water and forcing the stream to make a little loop. Some previous hikers must have passed this point, because three logs had been set across the stream as a crude bridge.

"I guess we'll have to cross," Quinten said, squinting through the fog of his glasses. "It makes no difference if we're on one side of the river or the other."

Martin looked at me. "Can you make it, Grandma?"

"I'll have to," I said with a sigh. "Give me a minute to rest."

"We have to keep moving," Butch urged.

"He doesn't expect us to be here," his father said. "We can afford a few minutes."

The others sat down. I did not, not trusting myself to be able to get up again. Instead, I walked slowly back and forth, trying to limber up my back. It had gotten a bit better. The pain had become bearable, and I had a bit more range of motion. I was still far from okay, though.

Quinten used his Swiss Army knife, which he had been gripping the entire time, to divide up his two apples. We ate them greedily.

"We should go," I said.

"I'll go with you, Grandma. We're both light. The logs will hold us."

I smiled and tried to tousle his hair, which I couldn't, since he was wearing his hood. I only succeeded in making my hand wet.

"You're being very brave and helpful. Your parents will be very proud when I tell them."

The look he gave me horrified me—disbelief coupled with a smile, as if he was humoring me. Did he think I wasn't going to make it? Did he think none of us would? The determined young man I had seen in him hours before had vanished, replaced by a tired, hungry, and scared boy who had to help his slow-moving grandmother across a log spanning a cold, deep stream.

I looked him in the eye. "We're going to make it."

"Sure we will, Grandma."

Butch came up to us. "Let me test it before you guys go. I'm the heaviest."

Butch walked across it with no problem. His father followed. The librarian had just about made it across when the log on the left side slipped a little. He let out a yelp, arms cartwheeling.

He didn't make it. He half fell, half jumped into the stream. Because his fall was somewhat controlled, he managed to leap for most of the rest of the distance, landing knee deep with a loud splash. Quinten stumbled, ending up waist deep before managing to control himself and stagger back out.

"I'm okay, I'm okay," he said. Fortunately, he hadn't lost his glasses, not that they did him much good.

"Do you have a dry pair of pants?" I asked.

"No. My other pair got wet yesterday."

From the look on his face, I could tell he understood the problem. With the temperature cooling and no sign of the rain letting up, he was at risk for hypothermia.

"Can you borrow a pair from Butch?"

He shook his head. "His spare pair got wet too."

"My other pants are mostly dry," Martin chimed in.

"They won't fit me," Quinten said.

So there was nothing we could do. We would have to forge on and hope for the best.

Butch and Quinten secured the log that had slipped as well as they could, and Martin hopped onto the crude bridge. He held out a hand for me, and I painfully stepped on. The logs were smooth and slick from the rain. If my back had been all right, I would have gotten on my hands and knees and crawled. That wasn't an option. If I tried that, I probably wouldn't have been able to get up again.

Slowly, we picked our way across, me using my spear to steady myself as best I could while dear little Martin took much of my weight. The boy and the Stone Age weapon made an odd pair of crutches. At least they got me across.

There was no trail on the opposite bank, but at least it was more or less level. We walked along, slumped and tired, Quinten squishing with every step. The woods to our right began to thin, and I could discern a gap in them before another line of trees took up the near distance. The gap drew closer as we walked, and I got a sinking feeling.

That feeling was confirmed a half mile downstream when another stream to our right angled in and joined the stream we had been following, bringing us to a halt on a spit of land.

"Now what do we do?" Martin cried.

Butch clutched his father, who sneezed.

Darn good question. My first thought was to go back and retrieve the logs and use them to make a bridge over this new barrier. That would add nearly a mile to our walk. At our level of fatigue, that wasn't a good idea. I studied the wooded landscape as much as I could in the poor visibility. We stood in a valley, broader than the one we had hiked up. There was no guarantee that we wouldn't come across another tributary to the main stream that would once again block our passage.

The other options were to go upstream, hoping to find a ford—unlikely with all this rain—or go back the way we came and try to find some other way out.

Martin cursed and sat on a rock. Butch kicked a stick into the river. Quinten was beginning to shiver. I glanced at my watch. It would be dark soon.

To my surprise, the librarian showed the most resolve.

"Why don't we go upstream and find some logs? We can make another bridge."

"What if we don't find any?" his son asked.

"We can check the opposite bank too. This other stream doesn't look any wider than the last one. Since I'm already wet anyway, I can wade across."

"All right, let's go upstream a bit," I said.

It took a minute to get the boys moving again. Both their stomachs had been growling for some time.

"Have a gummy bear each," I told them. "You need the sugar. But only one."

Just saying this depressed me. We were down to rationing gummy bears?

We moved upstream, all of us slower than before and moving directly opposite the way we should have been. I was beginning to wonder if we would even make it to the bridge at all.

I was also worried about Quinten. He kept sneezing. The great blasts sent birds flapping out of trees and startled squirrels scurrying away into the underbrush. He had obviously caught a cold the day before, and now that he was soaking wet with no way to dry off, he would only get worse.

Despite this, he didn't slow down or complain; he just kept walking and looking for a place to cross.

We trudged along for a good half hour before he suddenly stopped.

"There," he said, pointing across the stream.

Erosion had undercut a couple of smaller trees. They lay next to an older log that looked pretty rotten. The three of them together might make a halfway-decent bridge.

Maybe.

Except they were on the opposite bank.

"I'll wade across," Quinten said.

"You'll get soaked," I objected.

"I'm already soaked. The stream is less than ten feet wide. I won't be in the water for long."

"No, but you'll get even colder than you are now."

He shook his head. "No choice."

He was right. There was no choice.

The librarian began to wade out into the stream, letting out a great sneeze that sent ripples across the water. This stream turned out to be deeper than the other one, and the water rose past his waist, forcing him to pull off his coat and hike up his sweater and shirt so they wouldn't get wet.

When he got across, he laid his coat under a tree

and dragged one of the newly fallen trees across to us. As we secured the end to our side of the stream, sticking it into the mud and weighing it down with a couple of rocks, he went back for the next one. A third trip brought back the rotted old log. The water-logged, dead wood felt like putty in my hands.

"I think this will break under our weight," I said.

"Walk on the smaller logs and only use the old one to steady yourself," Quinten said.

I examined the smaller trees. Small and with slick bark. It would be quite a balancing act, and with my back, I wasn't sure I could do it.

But, as Quinten had pointed out, we had no choice.

"I'll help steady you," Quinten said. His voice came out dull, listless.

"No, you're shivering. Get to the far bank and put your raincoat back on."

His hair and sweater were already getting wet from the rain. Quinten hesitated for a second then nodded and waded back across the stream. I noticed his hands fumbled his coat as he tried to put it back on.

He was entering the first stages of hypothermia.

"Butch, you go across first and test it."

Neither of the kids had said anything during all

of this. They were getting worn out. I glanced at my watch. Sunset in less than two hours. The temperature would drop, and Quinten would be in serious trouble.

I worried about the rest of us too. Tired and with little food, what would we do at night? Sooner or later, one of us wouldn't be able to go on—most likely Quinten, followed closely by myself. My back still ached, although I had walked out some of the tension. I could handle it as long as it didn't get worse again. My real problem was fatigue. In our situation, there was no remedy for that.

A snap of wood brought me out of my worries and added a new one. Butch had been walking across the flimsy bridge, balancing on the two thin logs and avoiding the thick rotted one in between, when the left one snapped under his weight. He cursed as he fell, landing hard on his right knee as his left leg went all the way into the water. He crawled the rest of the way on the remaining two logs.

Great. Now father and son would both get hypothermia.

"I'll help you across, Grandma," Martin said, examining the log bridge with a dubious eye.

"I don't think it can take both of our weight. I'll go first, and then you go."

I got on my hands and knees. As painful as that was, I knew if I tried to walk across, I'd slip and wrench my back again. A third twist like that and I might be out of commission.

Every inch was agony, but I made it across. Martin came next, crawling like I did, as Quinten stamped his feet to get warm, teeth chattering.

"All right," I said with more determination than I felt. "Let's eat all the rest of the food and make a final push for the bridge."

"Let's eat while we walk," Quinten said and let out a loud sneeze. "I need to warm up."

"Can't we build a fire?" Butch asked, shaking his soaked leg. The poor boy looked like he had wet himself.

"Orrin would see the smoke," Martin said.

We set out, none too quickly. Within half an hour, the sky had grown visibly dimmer. The temperature had dropped as well. I estimated we had about an hour of daylight left.

At least the valley we were in ran relatively straight and level. Although there was no path, and Quinten was moving more and more slowly, shivering all the way, we were moving forward.

That wouldn't be enough. The librarian was beginning to lag behind, his eyes hooded, half-asleep on his feet. Drowsiness was another symptom of hypothermia. And Butch was complaining that he was cold too.

Once the sun set and the temperature cooled even further, father and son would be in serious trouble.

The stream curved around a rock promontory that we had to skirt and climb at an agonizingly slow pace.

"Let's take a break," Quinten said, stopping at the summit. His words came out slurred, another sign that he was losing core body temperature.

"We can't. If you stop moving, you won't get started again," I said. I nudged him along. He moved forward like an automaton.

As the others descended the far side of the promontory, something made me look back the way we had come.

Just in time to see someone run into the woods some distance behind us.

I only saw him for a second. That was enough. He was a burly man dressed in camouflage pants, a dark-brown hunter's jacket, and a broad-brimmed hat, rushing into the woods and out of sight. He looked to be about six foot two with short blonde hair. He appeared to be in his late thirties.

Orrin Hitt.

My heart hammering in my chest, I noticed something even worse: the logs from our bridge floating down the stream.

He had known we had come this way, perhaps intended it all along, and he had just gotten rid of our only escape route.

He was coming for us, and he'd catch us before long.

THIRTEEN

"He's coming," I said as I crested the hill and hurried down to join them.

The others turned and stared at me.

"He's followed us. He's on this side of the stream, and he's pulled away the bridge."

"We have to run!" Martin said, eyes growing wide.

"We can't outrun him." And by "we," I meant "me."

And Quinten. He was shaking like a leaf now.

I stopped and looked around. We were still high enough to see a fair amount of the surrounding countryside. The stream continued straight, as wide as ever, with a steady flow that told me that it had become deeper. To our right rose the side of the valley. Up ahead, there was a break in the trees where a little side stream splashed down the slope to join the main stream. Next to it, about two-thirds of the way up, I could see a little clearing in the trees. I couldn't see what was there, but I noticed the slope steepened at that point.

That gave me an idea.

"Let's go," I said. "We're going to give him the slip."

As soon as we got down the other side of the hill and were on the level again, I glanced back the way we had come. Our trail was not very clear, even to my trained eye. This close to the stream, there was little grass, and the only mark of our passage was the occasional bent-back bush or snapped twig. I wondered how good Orrin was at tracking.

Maybe he didn't know how. A simple hiker wouldn't, and if he was a hunter, he would have brought his rifle.

Those were pretty slim assumptions to bet my life on, but I'd done so before on slimmer assumptions.

"We're going up the side of the valley."

"My dad's getting tired," Butch said.

"It's only for a little way."

I spotted the perfect place to move off the trail:

another tumble of rocks where rivulets of water flowed down the valley side.

"Be very careful to step on only the rocks," I told them. "We don't want to leave a trail."

Martin and Butch leapt from rock to rock like mountain goats, their weariness torn away by fear. I had to pick my way more carefully. The rocks were slippery with rain. Quinten fell almost at once, picked himself up, then fell more seriously a hundred yards up the slope.

He got up slowly and trudged along, holding his wrist. As numb as he was, he must have smacked it pretty badly to feel it at all.

Covering up the marks he had made in the mud as well as I could, I told everyone to veer left.

"Where are we going?" Martin whined.

"I'm not sure, but if we're lucky, we'll get some-place where we can warm up and avoid Orrin."

We were in luck for once, and it turned out I was correct. After linking up with the stream I had spot-ted, we followed it uphill for a bit until we came across the opening to an old mine in a steep part of the slope. This was the clearing of trees I had seen from the hilltop. The miner had cut down trees immediately in front of the mine entrance, and only thin saplings had grown in their place.

Peering through the flimsy boards, I saw that one of the wooden posts about ten feet inside the entrance had collapsed, causing part of the roof and wall to give away. I beamed my flashlight past the pile of rubble and saw the rest of the tunnel wasn't in much better shape.

I turned to them. The boys looked at me eagerly, hoping I had a plan. Quinten stood slumped, eyes hooded, shivering and indifferent. He was too far gone to help much, and now that we had stopped, I wasn't sure I'd be able to get him moving again.

"Hopefully Orrin didn't notice we left the riverside. He'll assume we're following it out of the park like we have been all along. He's following a false trail now."

"But when he doesn't catch up to us, won't he figure out we climbed up the side of the valley?" Martin asked.

"He will, but he won't know where. That gives us some time. Everyone, take your packs off."

"Time to do what?" my grandson asked.

"To build a fire. We need to warm ourselves up."

As if to emphasize my point, Quinten let out a sneeze.

"Won't Orrin see the smoke?" Butch asked, echoing Martin's question from earlier.

"Not the way we're going to build it. Butch, tear these boards off. They're pretty dry thanks to the overhang. Oh, and pry out the nails. We'll want those. Be careful. Use a rock to tap on the sharp ends of the nails to drive them out of the wood. Martin, go see if you can find some kindling that's more or less dry. Don't stray out of sight."

We got the boards off quickly enough and piled them just inside the mine alongside a pile of rusty nails. Cautiously, I crept into the mine, eyeing the cracked and eroded ceiling as I did so. The support post had come entirely loose and lay on the floor, partially covered by fallen bits of the wall and ceiling.

"Quinten, come in here and fetch this." I said this in a whisper, as if my voice might make the whole place come down.

"I'll do it, Dad," Butch said.

"No, you break up the boards, and be careful with the nails. He needs to keep moving."

Butch's face grew serious. He must have figured out what was happening to his father.

Quinten fumbled to remove the stones, his movements clumsy. I gave him room and moved out of the mine, glancing all around. Martin was a few yards away, a bundle of sticks under his arm.

The clatter of falling rocks inside the mine made me spin around, a sharp pain going up my back at the sudden move.

Quinten stumbled out, covered in dust and holding his shoulder.

"What happened?" I asked.

"Dunno," Quinten mumbled.

I looked past him and saw some new rocks on the ground and a fresh bit of erosion on the wall. He must have banged against it.

I probed the wall with my spear. A few more flakes came off, but nothing major.

"Butch, your father managed to clear most of that debris away. See if you can pull that beam to the entrance."

Much as I hated putting him in danger, if we didn't get a good fire going, his father might be dead by morning.

Butch moved carefully into the mineshaft the ten feet it took him to get to the beam. He lifted it, checking all around him, then pulled it to the entrance where he had stacked the boards.

I should have had him do it in the first place. I'd been foolish to have a man suffering the clumsiness and drowsiness of hypothermia do such a dangerous job.

I should have had them pull away both the log bridges as well. Maybe Orrin wouldn't have known where we had gone. At least it would have slowed him down a bit.

Mistakes. A whole string of mistakes. Was I getting hypothermia too? I was cold and weary but didn't feel unusually so.

Unfortunately, the person with hypothermia was often the last to know about their state.

Martin came back with the kindling. "Sorry, it's all wet," he said. "I couldn't find any dry stuff anywhere."

"That's all right."

I used my survival knife to sharpen several of the longer sticks and had the boys use them as poles to set up the tarp over the entrance of the mine. Then I got them to pile up the leaves that had blown into the mine and had stayed dry. I added a roll of toilet paper to this heap and piled the broken boards on top. I lit the tinder and had Quinten use his spare shirt to flap at the fire. The breeze fanned the flames, and soon it was burning merrily.

"Keep flapping that shirt," I told the librarian. "You need to keep moving, and it will put most of the smoke into the mine instead of up in the air."

"Some's still going up in the sky, Grandma. Won't Orrin see?"

I studied the smoke that managed to drift out around the tarp. "It isn't much, and it's getting dark. Gray smoke against a gray sky? Hopefully he won't see."

"Gray smoke against green trees," he corrected.

"True enough, but we're not done yet. Butch, shove that beam so the end is pressed against the fire. It will catch and burn slowly. As it burns away, push it little by little into the fire. And keep feeding boards into the fire as long as they last. Oh, and put those sticks Martin gathered close in so they dry. You and your dad stay close to the fire, too, so that you'll warm up and get dry."

"What can I do, Grandma?" Martin asked.

"You and I are going to set some traps for Orrin."

He looked at me in disbelief.

I had him gather some sticks and sharpened them on both ends while he used one of the Swiss Army knives to hack away at the earth to make little pits the size of a man's boot. In each of these pits, we stuck a spike at the bottom and on the sides, then covered them with twigs and grass. We set these traps all around the perimeter except for the two routes that were the easiest to approach the mineshaft—a little gully to one side that angled up the slope to open out close to the mine entrance and the path we had taken directly across from the little stream.

Here, we got more creative. Cutting off the straps from the backpacks, I tied them end to end to fashion a rope. To one end, I tied a rock wrapped in a shirt with nails sticking out of it in all directions. I instructed Martin, my champion tree climber, to scurry up one of the trees and tie the other end of the rope to a branch. We then stretched out the rope with the spiked ball at the end and secured it to the crux of a branch on another tree with a few twigs.

Then I used some string I had in my survival pack as a tripwire to set across the path, running to the business end of my trap. If someone tripped over the wire, it would yank the twigs away that were holding the spiked ball, and it would swing down, hopefully hitting whoever approached our position. We made two such traps, one for each likely approach to the camp.

I say "we" and "I," but it was really Martin doing all the work under my instruction. I stood painfully on the sidelines, leaning against a tree, my forehead beaded with sweat thanks to the agony of my back.

Martin did everything he was told in stunned

silence. By the time we finished, it was fully dark, and we headed back to Quinten and Butch by the fire.

"You wouldn't believe what my grandma knows how to do!" Martin said, his eyes bright in the firelight. "We've set traps all over this place. Orrin better hope he doesn't find us. We'll get him for sure!"

I wished I shared his confidence. The traps were crude, and a shortage of nails meant there were enough gaps in our line that the killer might pass right through without setting off anything. But it was the only protection we had.

"How did you learn how to do all that stuff?" Butch asked. "Were you in the Special Forces or something?"

Martin turned to me. "Yeah. How do you know that stuff?"

"Never mind," I said in a quiet voice. "How are you feeling, Butch?"

"Better. My pants are dry. I stuck my wet leg real close to the fire like you said, and it dried pretty quick. I burned my shoelaces, though."

An honors student, to be sure.

I turned to his father. "And how are you feeling, Quinten?"

He had gotten into his sleeping bag and lay close

to the crackling fire. His wet pants and underwear were laid out by the fire, steam rising from them.

Quinten nodded wearily. "Better. Not shivering anymore. Tired, though."

"You just get some rest." I snapped my fingers. "Didn't you say you have some cornmeal in your pack?"

"Yeah."

I rummaged through his pack and found the cornmeal as well as a light frying pan I remembered him using. I instructed the boys to find a flat stone to put on top of the fire and set the pan on it. I mixed the cornmeal with a bit of water. Unfortunately, Ms. Chipper had the powdered milk, baking powder, sugar, oil, and everything else you need to make cornbread, but at least it would be edible. We were too hungry to be picky.

Pretty soon, I was stirring a lumpy mass resembling badly made polenta. It looked thoroughly unappetizing. Still, it was food. My stomach grumbled. Quinten's stomach grumbled. Martin's stomach grumbled. Butch drooled in a most disgusting manner.

Butch's head jerked to one side. His eyes went wide, staring out into the darkness. The drooling cut off sharply.

"What was that?" he whispered.

I set aside the spoon and picked up my spear. We were all looking out into the shadows now.

"You heard something?" I asked, my voice hushed.

Then I heard something, too, a faint rustling coming from the direction of the gully.

I took a few steps away from the fire, angling to the side so as to get into the shadow of the mine entrance. Since the fire was actually just inside the mine, I didn't have to go far before the darkness swallowed me.

Butch and Martin stayed where they were, Butch clutching his Swiss Army knife and Martin his big stick.

They looked vulnerable and very lonely in the flickering light of the fire, the only adult in sight lying listlessly in his sleeping bag.

I strained my ears, trying to catch any sounds above the crackling of the fire, the boys' heavy breathing, and the patter of rain.

There it was a again. A rustling of leaves. It was definitely coming from the gully.

And it sounded closer than last time.

FOURTEEN

We stood in silence, ears perked, eyes straining to see into the inky black of a rainy night.

I squeezed myself into the shadow cast by the edge of the mineshaft. The light from the fire cast a bright glow out into the night like a shimmering flashlight. In contrast to that, I should be invisible to whoever was coming up that gully.

I hoped.

The boys and Quinten remained in sight. I felt like screaming at them to get out of view, but it was too late. Orrin, assuming it was Orrin, would have spotted them by now. I was sure he didn't have a gun. That wasn't his style. He liked to crush people— Thomas with a blunt object smacked over and over again against his head and two attempts to crush us with falling rocks. This man didn't just want to kill people; he wanted to break them.

And that was what he wanted to do with us. With my grandson.

Not on my watch.

I gripped my spear, keeping it in my own shadow so the knife that made its business end wouldn't catch any reflections, and waited. I didn't even think about my back; all I thought about was protecting the people whose safety had become my responsibility.

Another rustle, much closer this time, then the sound of someone stumbling.

A whoosh in the air, a thud, and a cry.

Like some Paleolithic cavewoman, I raised my spear high, let out a yell, and charged down the hill to defend my young. A hundred thousand years of instinct burned through my veins, giving me the fighting instinct of a saber-toothed tiger.

The instinct, but not the ability.

I slipped on the wet grass and landed on my rear end, sending a spike of pain up my back. My war cry turned into a yelp. For a moment, I was paralyzed and could only sit there helpless, still clutching my spear but unable to use it.

Orrin staggered into view, emerging from the shadows into the firelight like some demonic vision.

He clutched his side, blood flowing freely through his fingers. His face was rigid with pain and rage. In his other hand, he gripped a hammer.

A *hammer*. What kind of psychopath takes a hammer on a hiking trip?

This psychopath. And now he was coming for us.

"Run!" Martin cried. I heard him and his friend rush off into the underbrush.

So much for adolescent bravado.

"Orrin Hitt," I said in an authoritative voice, "everyone knows it was you. You won't get away with this. You've already killed one man. That's going to give you years of prison time. You kill anyone else, and that's the electric chair."

When I say "authoritative voice," I mean a pained, warbling squeak.

Leveling my spear at him was probably more effective. I hoped my face didn't betray how painful even that simple movement was.

Still clutching his side from where my booby trap had hit him, he approached me. His gait grew steadier. While he was in pain and losing blood, rage gave him strength.

It became painfully obvious to me that I was not his match. Perhaps if my back hadn't been out, I could have taken him on. Perhaps if I had been fighting on a full stomach. Perhaps if I were ten years younger.

"Perhaps" wouldn't mean anything when he got within swinging distance with that hammer.

Time for a radical change of plan. Ignoring the pain in my back as much as I could, I let loose with one final effort. I reversed the grip on my spear, coiled up, and threw it at the dead center of his chest.

The pain almost knocked me out. My gasp mingled with his own. I looked up, my eyes half-shut, my head swimming, and I saw him stagger to the side, my crude spear stuck in his thigh.

A throw at a large man less than ten feet away, and I almost missed? I reminded myself not to get into fights after three-day hikes with a bad back.

Orrin snarled. With a jerk, he pulled the spear out of his thigh. He stood there a second, grinding his teeth, and then limped toward me.

Oh well. It all had to end sometime. At least the boys had gotten away.

A bellow from behind me made us both look. Quinten, wearing a shirt, his underwear, and nothing else, ran down the hill with the skillet in his hand. With a deft movement, he tossed the contents into

Orrin's face, who screamed and clutched at the half-burnt cornmeal.

Not for long. Quinten followed up with a swing of the frying pan at Orrin's head, connecting with a loud *clong*.

The evil janitor went down for the count.

Quinten stared at the motionless body at his feet. "Omigod, did I kill him?"

I could see Orrin breathing. "No."

"Whew! Uh-oh. We need to tie him up or something."

I pointed my flashlight down the gully, where the spiked ball hung at the end of the rope.

"Use your Swiss Army knife to cut that rope. You can use that."

"Righto." Quinten sneezed.

"Be careful of the spike traps. Stick to the center of the gully."

Quinten got back safely, still sneezing, and tied Orrin's hands behind his back, sneezing on him a couple of times. I hoped Orrin would catch his cold.

"Well done," I said. "You're shivering again. Get out of the rain and back into your sleeping bag."

I had managed to struggle to my feet. My back was a solid plank of pain, but I could move after a fashion, and Orrin was no longer a threat.

For the first time, Quinten noticed his own state of undress. He looked down at himself, yelped, and scurried back into the modest safety of his sleeping bag.

"Don't worry about it. At least you had your underwear on."

"It dried out quicker than my pants. I put it back on just before he showed up. It's nice and toasty now."

Too much information, as my grandson would say.

The boys!

"Martin! Butch!"

A rustle in the bushes, and two frightened faces poked out of the greenery and into view.

"We saw everything!" Butch said. "You were awesome, Dad!"

Quinten gave a thumbs-up from inside his sleeping bag.

"Those traps really got him!" Martin enthused. "And you even threw a spear. You're a badass, Grandma."

I basked in the admiration, as I'm sure Quinten did too. While there must have been easier ways to gain adolescent approval, I took what I could get.

"Careful with the pit traps!" I shouted as they approached the camp.

"Don't worry, Grandma. I'm the one who dug them, remember?"

I retrieved my spear, taking a good thirty seconds or so to bend down enough to grasp it and another thirty seconds to get back up.

Martin and Butch stood a little ways away, staring at Orrin. The janitor was just beginning to stir.

"Martin, go fetch my first aid kit. He's wounded, and I don't want him to bleed out before he sees a courtroom. I'm in no condition to patch him up, so you'll have to do it under my instructions."

"I don't want to touch him!"

"Do you want him to bleed to death in the rain?"

Martin hesitated then ran to get the first aid kit.

The boys propped Orrin against a tree, and Martin bound up the flowing wounds in his side and thigh. Then he put some anti-burn salve on Orrin's face.

The killer had woken up fully now and glared at us in silence.

"So why did you kill Thomas Cardiff?" I asked, pointing my spear at him.

His reply was unprintable.

"He got you fired, didn't he? He found something in your past, something reported in a newspaper in some town near to Cheerville. I'm thinking your name rang a bell. He remembered it in connection to some story that wasn't published in his own paper but that he had glimpsed a few years ago in a neighboring paper. So last month, he looked it up and got you canned. Why? You worked at the high school for several years, and he didn't do anything. What changed?"

Orrin glared at me. Even tied up and wounded, he was intimidating, and I was not easily intimidated. I was amazed the photography teacher had dared to take him on.

Orrin shrugged. "Maybe he recognized my name, and maybe he didn't. He never messed with me until I tried to get money off him."

"How?"

"He got into big trouble for going to the B&B. It's a—"

"Strip club. I know."

Martin gave me a scandalized look.

"Yeah, well, the school board told him if he ever went back, he'd get fired. Then I saw him there. I took a picture of him and told him I wanted five hundred bucks a month or I'd show it to the school board."

Great. Another employee of the public school system going to the local jiggle joint. The more I dug into the secrets of Cheerville, the less I liked what I found.

"Did he pay?" Quinten asked from his place beside the fire.

"The first month, yeah. That was just playing for time. I guess my name did ring a bell, because he found out I had a criminal record. Couple of cases of assault in Millersburg, where I used to live. Smacked around some people who didn't show me respect. Nobody messes with me."

"And Millersburg is where you got familiar with the outdoor shop. Go on. How did you get a job with the school system if you're a convicted violent criminal?"

He gave me an arrogant smile. "Easy. I got connections in the state government. Right at the top. I got my parole records wiped."

"Most likely you bribed or intimidated some low-level bureaucrat to wipe your records," I said. "It happens all the time. But you couldn't wipe the newspaper archive. Your distinct name gave you away. Thomas remembered reading your name in the Millersburg paper and looked you up."

"And that got him wondering why you weren't on parole," Quinten said. "That's why Thomas was looking at legal books—to check if you should be on parole or not. When he found out you were supposed to be, he put two and two together."

"Yeah, and got me fired!" Orrin snapped. "He figured that if he showed them that, they wouldn't care if he had been in the B&B. So they forgave him and fired me! You know how hard it is to get a job these days?"

While it unsettled me that they had continued to let Thomas teach, he had revealed that a criminal with a violent past was working in the school. That was more important than some little suburban peccadillo.

I shook my head in disgust. "So you decided on revenge. You couldn't stand losing a job you shouldn't have had in the first place. Even worse, you couldn't stand being outsmarted. But murder, Orrin? You were willing to actually kill for this?"

Orrin sneered. "He didn't show me any respect. I told you, nobody messes with me."

"What was the burning H for?" I asked.

The firelight shone like an evil gleam in his eye.

"I wanted him to know. I wanted him to fear me. Live with it for a day before I offed him."

"But he managed to photograph you. So you snuck into camp and stole his camera. What did you take out of his wallet?"

"A memory card. Those are both gone. You'll never find them."

"Perhaps not. It doesn't matter. What happened the night you killed him? He went out to confront you."

"He heard me close to your camp. He came out to offer me a bribe and threaten me with those pictures. It was too late for all that. I bashed his head in."

"Did the others get away?" Martin asked. He stood with Butch a few yards away, staring in wonder at the man they had only known as a humble janitor, now grown in stature to a ruthless killer.

Orrin fixed those baleful eyes on my grandson, who took a step back.

"Yeah, I couldn't stop everyone. I came after you because you were nosing around my camp."

"You wanted to clean up the evidence and get rid of us," I said. "That still wouldn't have covered your tracks. They would have proven it was you sooner or later."

"I don't like people nosing into my business."

"Like Thomas. You bashed his head in with that hammer for nosing into your business." My anger rose. "And you would have done the same to me and Quinten. And then you would have smashed the skulls of two fourteen-year-old boys. You would have killed two innocent children just for being in the wrong place at the wrong time."

I stepped forward and pressed the tip of my spear against his throat.

"You're lucky I'm one of the good guys."

The *chop chop chop* of a helicopter cut through the night. It grew louder, joined by the sounds of two or three others. Distant spotlights beamed down from the sky onto the valley about a mile away.

"That must be the police!" Martin said. "Butch, help me pull the tarp away so they can see the fire."

The boys ran off. I remained where I was, the tip of my spear poking Orrin's throat.

He gave me a mocking smile. "You're not going to do it, are you? If someone threatened someone I cared about, I'd bash their heads in."

"I seriously doubt you care about anyone."

"No one crosses me without getting hurt. Go on. Do it. No one's watching. You can say I lunged at you and you defended yourself. Everyone will believe you. No? Coward. I knew you wouldn't do it."

I glared at him. "I'm one of the good guys. I told you."

"One of the weak."

"Says the man who never rose above janitor and who will now be mopping a jail cell instead of a school until he's an old man. If I'm one of the weak, why did I beat you? Me and a librarian and two boys? You're not some rugged individual, some misunderstood genius. You're just a thug and a loser. You're not even that good a criminal. Now, if you'll excuse me, I think I'll go join someone who loves me and watch the helicopters come in."

I turned my back on him and walked back up the hill.

The boys had torn away the tarp so that the fire was more visible from the sky. The helicopters immediately turned and came in our direction. Martin and Butch cheered, jumping up and down and waving. Quinten sat up in his sleeping bag and waved too.

"We did it! We're safe!" Butch cried.

"You did it, Grandma," Martin said, giving me a hug.

"Well, you certainly helped."

Martin's face fell. "I ran. Me and Butch. We left you guys alone to face Orrin."

I gave him a hug. "You've been very brave through all of this. You helped me across the bridges, and you helped me set the traps. You can't be expected to face a maniac with a hammer."

"You did."

"I have lots of experience."

I hadn't meant to say that. It just slipped out.

Martin looked at me quizzically. "What did you really do for the government, anyway?"

I was saved from having to answer by the thunderous approach of the helicopters. A search beam blazed down on us.

"THIS IS THE POLICE. STAY WHERE YOU ARE," a loudspeaker blared. "WE ARE COMING TO SAVE YOU."

The lead helicopter hovered directly overhead, its searchlight blinding us like some UFO about to beam us aboard. From out of this light came a pair of human silhouettes, rappelling down from the helicopter. Two SWAT team members in full Kevlar and assault rifles thumped to the ground next to us. I dropped my spear in case they got trigger happy.

"Stay where you are!" one shouted. "We'll clear the area!"

"We already have," Martin said.

They ignored him. More SWAT team members rappelled down to our position, descending by pairs in rapid succession.

"Cool!" Butch said.

"The murderer is tied up over there," I shouted over the hammering of the helicopter and the cops screaming orders at each other. They ignored me.

"Move out!" their commander called.

A dozen bulky men and women charged down the slope.

"Wait!" I cried. "The forest is booby trapped!"

As if on cue, three of them stepped into my pit traps all at once and fell down.

"They're firing at us!" one of the fallen said.

"No one shot you," I said. "It's—"

"Return fire!"

The SWAT team began firing into the woods. A series of repeated flashes sparked from the helicopters as snipers join in.

A hulking man let out a battle cry and ran past me toward the stream.

"Not that way! I've set—"

He set off the trip wire. The ball of spikes swung down and implanted itself in his back armor.

"He's got me!" the cop shouted, spraying the

shrubs on full auto. Leaves and branches flew everywhere. He even managed to shoot the rope of the trap, leaving the ball of spikes stuck in his back.

Through all this, Orrin sat, amazed, staring at the leafy carnage all around him. No one paid him the slightest attention.

As the guns blared, another figure came rappelling down out of the light. I immediately recognized the plump silhouette of Cheerville Chief of Police Arnold Grimal. The harness had hitched up his belly to make it look like a single large breast. He spun at the end of the line, waving his arms and legs like a spider on too much caffeine, and thumped to the ground in a heap. I went over and unclipped him.

"Ugh. You again," he said. I could barely hear him over the gunfire.

"The perp is over there. Get your friends to stop firing before they kill every tree out here. I know a local P.E. teacher who will turn you in if you're not careful."

Grimal slumped off down the slope, waving his arms and screaming for everyone to stop. It took him some time to be heard.

"I got the perp right here," he announced, slapping cuffs on Orrin's wrists even though they were already tied together. "He was working alone."

"Then what about the platoon that was firing at us?" a Kevlar-clad behemoth asked.

"There is no platoon. You were firing at trees, you idiot."

I cringed. Hearing Grimal calling someone an idiot had to be the worst insult ever.

The firing died down as the SWAT team slowly began to realize that Grimal was right and there weren't any perps out there firing back at them.

"Don't worry, lady. We've secured the area," one of them told me. He still had my spiked ball stuck in his back armor. I decided to leave it there.

I was relieved to see that the three who had fallen into my pit traps weren't hurt. Their boots had been tough enough to resist the wooden spikes.

Still, Martin was quite proud of himself.

"We took out a whole SWAT team, Grandma."

I smiled and put my fingers to my lips. "Sometimes it's best not to brag about your achievements."

We were evacuated to the nearest police station, where we were reunited with the rest of the group, who sat in a conference room, drinking coffee and eating donuts. The four of us dove for the donuts.

Grimal almost pushed me to the floor to get a couple for himself.

The next few minutes were a cacophony of enthusiastic teenagers sharing their adventures. Soon, Martin took center stage.

"And then we built traps for him! We made pits with spikes in them and swinging spike balls and everything! He tripped on one and got a spiked ball stuck right in him. Then my grandma and Butch's dad fought him off."

Martin got peppered with eager questions and was urged to repeat the story again, elaborating on the details. Everyone looked at him with a mixture of amazement and admiration.

Melanie most of all.

It looked like M&M would become an item.

The excitement soon waned, replaced by heavy fatigue. Within half an hour, we were in police cars, being driven back to the parking lot to pick up our own vehicles.

Martin sat in the back seat of a patrol car with me, his eyes hooded with sleepiness.

"We should go hiking again sometime," Martin mumbled half to himself.

I blinked with surprise. "Really? After all the

horrible things we went through, I thought you'd never set foot off of pavement again."

He opened his eyes and looked at me with a laugh. "Come on, it's not like you're going to get involved in a *second* murder. What are the chances?"

I gave him a big hug and a kiss.

Oh, Martin, you innocent!

ABOUT THE AUTHOR

Harper Lin is a *USA TODAY* bestselling cozy mystery author. When she's not reading or writing mysteries, she loves going to yoga classes, hiking, and hanging out with her family and friends.

For a complete list of her books by series, visit her website.

www.HarperLin.com